Seeds From My Garden

Seeds From My Garden

Ginger Schmidt

iUniverse, Inc.
New York   Bloomington

Seeds From My Garden

Copyright © 2009 by Ginger Schmidt

Photography by Glen Shellhammer
Cover design by Glen Shellhammer
Foreword by James A. Langdoc

iUniverse books may be ordered through booksellers or by contacting:

iUniverse
1663 Liberty Drive
Bloomington, IN 47403
www.iuniverse.com
1-800-Authors (1-800-288-4677)

ISBN: 978-1-4401-5877-3 (sc)
ISBN: 978-1-4401-5878-0 (ebook)

Printed in the United States of America
iUniverse rev. date: 7/31/2009

Also by Bob and Ginger Schmidt

Great Lakes Circle Tour:

Reliving History Along Lake Michigan's Circle Tour Route

Great Lakes Camping:

A Complete Guide to More Than 750 Campgrounds in

Minnesota, Wisconsin and Michigan

To Bob Schmidt, author and devoted husband,
who wrote…

For a brief moment in time,

The Earth is ours —

Not to waste or own,

But to share with creatures

great and small.

Mission Statement,
Illinois Conservation Foundation,

Bob Schmidt, 2001

Acknowledgments

This book is the result of many years of God speaking to one if his servants. However, it would never have come to fruition without the encouragement and assistance of many of God's people.

I am deeply grateful for the dedication and hard work of my friend, photographer and graphic artist, Glen Shellhammer, for searching out and photographing flora and fauna in Florida, for the cover design, as well as for hours of proof reading.

I cherish the friendship, spiritual advice and encouragement of the Rev. James Langdoc, M. Div., who wrote the Foreword; and the Reverends David and Linda Jones, the Reverend Dan Smith, the Reverend Amy Manierre and the Rev. James Kuh, my son, who critiqued this manuscript.

To Clint McVickers for providing the setting for the cover photo at his Clint's Customs shop, I am most grateful.

Many hours of assistance in plant research were received from South Florida Cactus and Succulent Society, Doral, Florida;

Mounts Botanical Gardens, West Palm Beach, Florida; Klehm Arboretum and Botanical Gardens, Rockford, Illinois; Archbold Biological Station, Lake Placid, Florida; Highland Hammock State Park, Sebring, Florida; Wayne Belson, Split Oak Forest Mitigation Park, Kissimmee, Florida and Brad Kolhoff, Florida Fish and Wildlife.

To fellow authors, Prudy Taylor Board and David Kohn, and Emory Massman, Jr. for their constant encouragement and friendship, I am deeply grateful.

Foreword

Following almost four decades serving as a pastor in various settings in the United Church of Christ, it is no longer possible for me to number the times that individuals have told me that they "meet God" or "feel closest to God" while out in nature. Inasmuch as a number of those folks were church members that rarely gathered with the community of faith for worship or other activities but found plentiful time for golf, camping, boating and/or hunting, it seemed a sure bet that God must have been in the business of making outdoor "house calls." To tell the truth, I never presumed to know for sure which persons were sincere and which were dishonest with me and possibly with themselves.

Ginger Schmidt surely does "meet God" in the natural world and this, her new publication, is testimony to the reality of her experience. Her devotion both to gardening and to God, with whom she has been in a life-long and vital relationship, is clearly evident in this volume. A member of Emmanuel United Church of Christ in Sebring, Florida, where I am currently serving as the Interim Pastor, Ginger has written a book filled with reflections that it is a privilege to commend to others who may discover through her eyes and words a fresh, new pathway to spiritual discovery and reflection that will be personally enriching.

Seeds From My Garden is an affirmation of the wisdom proclaimed by the Hebrew psalmist: "The earth is the Lord's and the fullness thereof…" (Psalm 24:1)

James A. Langdoc

Seeds From My Garden

Introduction

God is still speaking! Sometimes we hear but we don't listen.

God wants to have a relationship with each of us, and we each feel his presence at different times. For some God is closest when they are studying His Word, or when they are performing acts of service. Still others hear his voice during times of worship and contemplation, but for me God grabs my attention when I find myself a small and imperfect creature in his great and prefect creation.

Seeds From My Garden is an attempt to share God speaking to one amateur gardener as He shows his Love, Faith, Patience and Joy to her life.

It is not the purpose of these devotions to present great theological theories or questions, but to assure you that God is closer than you think…

It all began with a few seeds; I planted as a four-year-old, brought from a visit to a Georgia cotton field. They grew, flowered and produced cotton, and I was hooked on gardening.

During World War II, my victory garden produced one serving of peas and seven string beans. In my college dorm room, I cultivated an air plant that flourished pinned to our drapes, until my roommate demanded its removal. Over the years, I've tended my tomato patches, rose gardens and patio pot gardens.

Some of the seeds I've planted withered and died, other were too crowded and had to be transplanted, but all brought forth a reminder that the seeds the Gardner has planted in me are still awaiting his harvest.

Seeds From My Garden takes you on a walk through backyards, along rivers and streams and down wooded lanes to observe the residents, both flora and fauna, of God's beautiful creation.

These personal experiences have brought me into a closer walk with God, and my prayer is that they will help you to hear God speaking to you and guiding you to cultivate the seeds he has planted in you.

Ginger Schmidt

Seeds of Love

All the special gifts and powers from God will someday come to an end, But love goes on forever.

I Corinthians 13:8 *LB*

No one has ever seen God, but if we love one another, God lives in us and his love is made complete in us.

I John 4: 12 NIV

My grandmother had few material possessions— her German Bible and hymnal, which she read and sang from constantly, and her sewing machine. However, if you asked her, she would tell you about all her great wealth — her family. Not just her three children, and many brothers and sisters, but all the townsfolk. Everyone who walked across her threshold was her family. She loved them, and they all loved her.

Left as a young woman with three small children to raise and only able to read and write in German, she depended on God for guidance and strength and for her sewing machine to put food on their table.

She made the wedding gowns and confirmation dresses for everyone in her small Michigan town and made the necessary alterations on all their garments as they changed in size and shape. Everyone in town lovingly called her "Grandma Rickie," which was short for Friederike Katherine.

Grandma's little house was the welcoming center of town and no one who entered ever went away hungry, even when the potatoes had to be divided again and the gravy thinned.

Living fifteen hundred miles away, my once-a-year visit with my grandmother was a royal event. Each year there was something new and unforgettable to learn. There were donuts to make, paper dolls to cut from her pattern books, and tin can stilts to master. She was never too busy to teach me a song in German, or tell me a story about when she was a little girl while she continued her sewing. Yet, what I recall most vividly is the summer I stripped her hollyhock plants of most of their beautiful blossoms.

Grandma had the most beautiful hollyhocks in town. They were every color of the rainbow and reached to the top of the backyard privy. Wanting to give my grandma a gift, I picked some of the most beautiful blossoms and excitedly ran into the house to present them— no stems, no leaves, just blossoms. As I plopped several handfuls down on the kitchen table, she first frowned, then smiled and hugged me saying,

"My, they are beautiful, but with no stems to hold them in a vase, we'll have to make dancing dolls."

Returning from her sewing machine with her pincushion, she got down her best, large relish dish, filled it with water and placed it in the middle of the table. Together we turned the colorful blossoms into ladies dressed in frilly skirts of pink, purple, red and white, and topped them off with floppy hats. One by one we placed them in the bowl and watched them float by each other as the warm breeze of a summer day filled the room.

One rainy-day many years later, when my young son begged me to put down my sewing and help him construct a cardboard-box train, I recalled how my grandma had sacrificed a morning of sewing to turn my flower-picking disaster into a gift of love. Together that day, my son and I made a real streamline engine.

Prayer: *Lord, You have given us such an abundance of your love. Make us ever mindful that it was given to share and that the more we share the more it will return to us.*

Hollyhocks

Years ago, because their height sometimes reached more than six feet, **hollyhocks** often joined sunflowers as a regular decoration surrounding buildings that housed the outdoor plumbing.

Hollyhocks are biennials or short-lived perennials that comprise the largest part of the flowering plants in the genus *Alcea* belonging to the mallow family *Malvaceae*.

For about two months in mid-summer, they produce large, saucer-shaped waxy blossoms in dark purple, red, pink, yellow and white. The double peony-like blossoms have become very popular, adding great beauty to garden borders. The "Charters Double" is so large and full that it resembles a pom-pom. The *Alcea rosea*, "Nigra," is one of the most beautiful and unique of all hollyhocks, and was grown by Thomas Jefferson at Montecello for its dark red, almost black flowers.

Hollyhocks grow easily from seed or seedlings and many

7

gardeners collect seed from one year to plant the next year. The plants are drought resistant and do well in the bright sunlight.

Believed to be native to Asia, hollyhocks appear in artwork from both China and Japan. The name, originally spelled "holihoc," comes from holi, or holy, and hoc, meaning mallow or plants with hairy stems and leaves. It has also been referred to as "St. Cuthbert's Cole," suggesting that it may have been found in the gardens of churches and monasteries. It is still a regular in English cottage gardens to provide a tall wall of color. European visitors to the Middle East brought the seeds home with them around the eleventh century; the seeds also have been recorded as cargo to the Americas. Although not as popular in today's gardens, they are still a regular in wildflower gardens. Because they easily reseed themselves, they are still frequently found along the fences of homes in rural areas.

Beloved, let us love one another, because love is from God; everyone who loves is born of God and knows God.

I John 4:7 NRSV

It was a hot, sweltering summer Sunday. Strains of "O Perfect Love" could be heard above the drone of the oscillating fans as a handful of people filed into our church sanctuary.

Wartime weddings were both joyous and sad times. Although

two young people were declaring their love for each other, family and friends were rarely able to attend.

Young brides, dressed in their Sunday best or a borrowed wedding gown, walked arm-in-arm with their boyish-looking grooms, attired in army khaki or navy white. Before a small gathering they would say their vows, promising to love until death might part them. There had been no time for parties, and a snapshot taken with someone's Kodak Brownie would be the official recording of their wedding.

Our choir director was committed to making this day a special day, just as it would have been back in the couple's hometown. She organized the ladies of the church to bake the wedding cake; she set an elegant table and even served the punch. She served as organist and soloist and florist as she decorated the church. Money was tight and supplies were scarce in our small southern town surrounded by three military bases. However, she made corsages and bouquets from oleander, jasmine and even periwinkles that outshined the artistic skills of any florist in town. Yet it was the altar flowers that I still see every time I tend the hibiscus in my garden.

In a basket, she would arrange a large spray of Carissa, a shiny green-leafed hedge plant that prides itself on having oversized sharp thorns. Usually these thorns an object of much complaining from gardeners when stabbed while trimming their hedges, but not this day. They were the apparatus upon which she arranged the beautiful showy hibiscus blossoms. Lovingly, she produced arrangements in shades of reds and pink, with the tiny white flowers of the Carissa adding to the overall beauty.

Few people knew that our wedding planner had studied at Julliard School of Music and appeared in operas across the country. On this day her center stage was a small church sanctuary, and her role was mother to our nation's war brides and their brave young grooms.

Over the years, I've decorated with hibiscus, my favorite flower. More than once, I've filled a swimming pool with these colorful blossoms for a luau or floated them in a bowl for a table centerpiece. I've even used them to help decorate my church sanctuary for special occasions. But never were they more beautiful than when those loving hands combined the splendor of the hibiscus blossom with the strength of the Carissa branches to celebrate the union of two young people in love.

Prayer: *Lord, Teach us to use our talents and time to show your love to others. Help us understand that it is not who we are, but what we do that will be of service to you.*

Hibiscus and Carissa

Hibiscus, or rosemallow, is a flowering tropical plant and a member of the *Malvacceae* family which also includes cocoa, cotton, okra and baobab.

The more than 200 species of this beautiful plant grow in warm temperate, subtropical and tropical regions throughout the world. Hibiscus is both an annual and a perennial plant and develops into both a woody shrub and a tree.

The blossoms are open bell-shaped flowers made up of usually five overlapping petals transitioning to a darker color near the center. A central column of fused stamens branch out at the end with a velvety stigma which only adds to the elegance of these blossoms.

Seven species of hibiscus are considered native to our island state and are known as Hawaiian hibiscus. *Hibiscus brackenridgei,* or *mao hau hele,* has bright yellow flowers and most often grows three to fifteen feet tall. The blossoms are usually four to six inches in diameter and appear daily between 2:00 and 4:00 P.M. and close about seven hours later. Although it is the state flower of Hawaii, it is currently on their endangered plant list.

When arriving on one of the islands, your plane will probably be greeted by Hawaiian girls in native costumes with a single hibiscus tucked behind their ears. The ear chosen for this adornment indicates their availability for marriage.

Island residents are not the only people to enjoy this lovely flower. It also grows in abundance in southern Florida where their bright yellow, salmon, red, pink and even gray, beige and white blossoms not only light up any garden but attract the birds, bees and butterflies.

In addition to their decorative qualities, some hibiscus have great value as a vegetable, as an ingredient in herbal teas, jams and even in hair care products. The *Hibiscus cannabinus* also known as Kenaf, is used in paper making.

Carissa grandiflora, or natal plum, although native to South Africa is very popular in Florida.

It is often used by oceanside homes because of its resistance to salt spray and because it is not easily damaged by wind. These plants may grow to a height of fifteen feet. They are also quite resistant to frost damage and can be found throughout South and Central Florida.

They make a great protective barrier with their thick shiny dark green leaves and sharp branched thorns. They are often planted beneath the windows of homes as a deterrent to burglars.

Throughout most of the year these plants produce a small five-lobed, white flower with a delicate fragrance resembling a gardenia.

Many varieties produce a oval-shaped reddish fruit. Although many gardeners leave the fruit for the birds to eat, others find the taste to be similar to that of cranberries and use it for sauces, jellies and even ice cream.

...I trust in God's unfailing love forever and ever.

Psalm 52:8 *NIV*

I glanced around my classroom. It was a typical classroom -- black chalkboards lined three walls; seven windows shaded by a huge holly tree offered both light and our only air conditioning. The back corner housed freshly painted radiators to provide warmth on occasional chilly Florida days.

An old oak teacher's desk stood as a sentry near the door, and thirty-six outdated student desks with empty inkwells (thank goodness) were lined up in silent rows.

In the 1950s classrooms all came with the same standard equipment — one hand-cranked pencil sharpener, a set of pull-down U.S. and World maps, a globe, several chalkboard erasers, a small cork bulletin board and a somewhat water-stained photo of George Washington crossing the Delaware.

I had spent one week trying to prepare my room for my first class. With "Welcome to Fourth Grade" pasted across the chalkboard, the names of my students taped to the door and on my desk, a vase of yellow and orange gaillardias "borrowed" from my neighbor's yard, I began greeting each student as they filed through the door and selected a seat. Finally I closed the door, took a deep breath and turned around to view every desk occupied and five students left standing in the back of the room. Quickly I assigned each to a place— one at my desk, several at work tables in the back of the room and even one whom I perched on a radiator. After nervously introducing myself and assuring them that I wanted to get to know each of them, I quickly handed a sheet of paper to each student and instructed them to get out their pencils. Because most of them were unsharpened, that gave me time to dig deep into my bag of inexperience and to come up with a topic for their first composition.

Outside the window I noted a holly tree, the only thing that was standing firm, calm and ready for whatever the day might bring. When all my charges were settled and staring at me with eager anticipation, I gave the command, "Now I want you to look out the window at the holly tree that will be our shade and friend this year, and make a list of things that you would do if you had that tree in your front yard." One by one the heads dropped as they began to write, and I dashed to the office down the hall to announce that I needed five more desks— P.D.Q.

Finally the desks arrived and when all the students had their battle station for the year, we proceeded with my planned first-day assignments.

When the dismissal bell rang and each had filed past me to receive their first hug, I finally sat down at my desk and checked my detailed lesson plans to see if we had accomplished all my daily goals. The stack of papers containing their first writing assignment of the year caught my eye and I began to read…."If I had the big holly tree in my front yard I'd…… There were the usual replies —"climb it," "water it," "care for it," — but one grabbed my attention. It was a neatly written response from a little boy who had sat very quietly near the back of the room. "I'd hug it. I'd try to see if I could get my arms all the way around it and give it a big hug."

It took several months before this little fellow began to sing with the group, volunteer to respond to questions, or even say a daily good-morning and good-bye. This behavior was difficult to understand until the first parent conference revealed that his father had been killed during the summer when the plane that he was piloting had exploded during an in-flight refueling exercise.

During the year, I often observed this little fellow leaning against our tree at recess or just staring at it, as if he needed the reassurance that it was still there.

It brought joy to all of us that year. By Christmas it decorated itself with tiny red berries. It was the stage for an occasional songbird's performance, our umbrella for outdoor story time; and it provided the only shade from the stifling afternoon heat as the year came to an end.

We learned many lessons that year. We learned to multiply with two numbers, to write a short story and to get to know and understand each other as we worked together. I learned that I didn't have to know the answers to all their questions, I only had to lead them to find their own answers.

Our tree was there for us every day— on sunny days and rainy days, happy days and sad days; and for one little boy being there brought back a smile and a laugh and the reassurance that it would always be there.

Prayer: *Father, hold us in your arms, let us lean on you when we are weak. Help us to stand tall and grow in your love, knowing that you will always be there with us.*

Holly Tree

Hollies, members of the *Aquifoliaceae* family are found as both trees and shrubs.

The American holly (*Ilex opa*) is found from New England to Florida and westward to Texas. Because they are dioecious (male and female), the male and female trees need to be planted in close proximity to produce berries. However, one male tree is enough for several female trees.

The American holly tree can grow to heights of fifty feet with a pyramid shape. The tree is best known for its leaves and berries which have become synonymous with Christmas. The thick, green, glossy leaves that are edged with stout prickles, alternately pointing upwards and downwards, tend to be found near the bottom of the tree with upper leaves rounder having only a single prickle.

In May the trees flower with a blossom that is pale pink on the outside and pure white inside. The female flowers are in groups of three to nine while the male flowers have only about one to three in each group. The flowers produce clusters of red berries, or drupes that have a stone-like seed inside the fruit. These are a favorite food of birds and animals.

The holly trees that are native to Florida are *Ilex cassine* or Dahoon holly. These trees reach heights of thirty feet and are often found in wet locations. An evergreen in warm climates, they shed their leaves in colder areas. One of the greatest differences between the American and Dahoon holly are the leaves. The Dahoon leaves are smoother, with only a few sharp teeth and a sharp bristle at the tip. Although not grown for its ornamental value, it is a beautiful tree with thick dark green foliage and attractive berries which are a food source for many songbirds.

Throughout the ages there have been a number of medicinal uses for both the leaves and berries. The leaves have been used to cure fevers, rheumatism and even smallpox, while the berries, although somewhat poisonous were thought to be useful in the treatment of dropsy (edema) and as an astringent.

The decorative leaves and berries are not the tree's only claim to fame. The hard, white, heavy wood of the tree is used for ornamental woodworking, and during the 1800s it was widely used for looms.

Linked with ivy in the lovely Christmas carol, "The Holly and the Ivy," the prickly leaves represent the crown of thorns worn by Jesus before his crucifixion, and the berries the drops of blood he shed.

Whether an American or a Dahoon holly, this tree is tall, stately and festive at all seasons.

Be on your guard; stand firm in the faith; be men of courage; be strong. Do everything in love.

I Corinthians 16: 13–14 *NIV*

Talk to anyone who is "from" Chicago and they'll tell you it is the "best town in America." Talk to anyone living in Chicago and they'll tell you where the best place is to go to get away from Chicago for the weekend. For us it was Rockford, Illinois.

Our travel trailer stayed parked in a secluded campground in a wooded valley about ninety miles northwest of Chicago, and every weekend from April 15th to October 15th we lived at Blackhawk Valley Campground.

By working an extra half hour each day, I was able to leave work two hours early, which meant beating the heavy exodus from the city to the country each weekend.

When my husband picked me up from work and after giving him and the dog a kiss (in that order), we were off for a weekend away from the sounds of the city and where the only sounds to be enjoyed were the wind in the trees and the laughter of fellow campers.

We enjoyed exchanging the confinement of our offices for the freedom of the outdoors. With no schedules to keep or deadlines to make, we strolled about the campground stopping to visit with friends or venturing up the path onto country lanes that encompassed the park.

One very warm summer day, we decided to wander a dirt path leading away from the campground. My husband, with camera in hand, and I, with Schatze, our spoiled dachshund in tow, went exploring. We wandered past a field of hay toward an old dilapidated barn, Bob snapping photos right and left and Schatze chasing butterflies in circles. Suddenly Bob froze in his tracks, staring ahead almost in a trance. When I arrived to investigate his find, there stretched before us was a field of poppies. Their brilliant red heads, perched at the ends of tall spindly stems, swayed in the breeze as if beaconing us to come nearer. Bob began to snap photos with gunshot speed, but the dog and I stood in reverent silence gazing at this field of glory.

Many times I had read to my students the words of Lt. Col. John McCrae's great poem, "In Flanders Fields," pointing out the poetic form of sonnet writing and the rhythmic sound of the iambic tetrameter, but never did I really think about Flanders Fields or even why poppies were sold on the street corners for Poppy Day.

When my husband finished photographing, this awesome

moment seemed to end, and we ventured back to the campground for lunch. However, the sight of that field of poppies remained in my memory. Back in our home office, I reread the lines of that memorable poem:

> In Flanders Field the poppies blow
>
> Between the crosses row on row,
>
> That mark our place; and in the sky
>
> The larks, still bravely singing, fly
>
> Scarce heard amid the guns below.
>
> We are the Dead. Short days ago
>
> We lived, felt dawn, saw sunset glow,
>
> Loved and were loved, and now we lie
>
> In Flanders fields.

I could somehow imagine how McCrae must have felt when sitting on the back of an ambulance, where he penned these words. He was a surgeon, attached to the First Field Artillery Brigade serving in the Ypres, Belgium, the scene of some of the biggest battles of World War I. On this day, in absence of the chaplain, he had just performed the funeral service for a young friend who was laid to rest amid a field of poppies, next to his dressing station.

The blood-red poppies I had viewed seemed to be reaching

upward as they swayed together. As if in cadence they whispered, "Remember me, remember me."

I recalled, when as a young girl, our pastor began our Wednesday evening prayer meeting, announcing in a hushed voice that they had just received word their oldest son had been called home to be with his Lord while landing on a beach in Normandy. A prayerful silence fell across the room as we bowed in prayer, remembering his sacrifice and the sacrifice of all our fighting forces *for peace and for our hope of "One World —God's World."*

Prayer: *Lord, You sent Jesus to show us Love, and Peace and Hope, and yet we continue to war against each other. Teach us to lay down all distrust and hatred and reach out to our brothers and sisters everywhere in love.*

Poppy

On their way to the Emerald City, do you remember how Dorothy, the Scarecrow, the Tin Man and the Cowardly Lion walked through a field of poppies and mysteriously Dorothy and the lion fell asleep? The poppies were the culprits. Over the years, poppies have been a symbol of sleep and death because of the opium extracted from them.

The beautiful, colorful *Papaver rhoeas*, field or corn poppy, is a plant with one blossom per stem. It is found as an attractive wildflower in fields or is cultivated as a border in gardens and as an accent in rock gardens.

The blossoms are white, pink, orange, red, blue and the California yellow, which has become their state flower. The center of the flower has a whorl of stamens surrounded by four to six cup-shaped petals.

Although well-known for their opium alkaloids used in the

making of morphine and codeine, its seeds have many culinary uses as a flavoring or as the topping to everyone's favorite, poppy seed rolls.

Poppies have become a symbol of wartime remembrance since the mid-1900s. The publishing in 1915 of John McCrae's famous poem, "In Flanders Field," created an emotional tribute to the sacrifice of those who have served their country. In 1922 the Veterans of Foreign Wars (VFW) launched the first distribution of poppies before Memorial Day and the poppy soon became their official memorial flower.

In Canada, poppies are distributed by the Royal Canadian Legion and Anavets each fall just before their Remembrance Day. Their poppy is constructed of red plastic with a felt lining and black center. In 1980 it was decided to change the center to green to represent the green fields of France. This proved rather unpopular and it has officially returned to the traditional black center.

Whether we view the stately poppy in an open field, as an accent to our rock garden, or pinned to the label of our jacket, the blood-red poppy always stirs our emotions in remembrance of the sacrifice of generations of men and women who have fought for peace in our world.

*You did not choose me, but I chose you and appointed
you to go and bear fruit—fruit that will last. Then the
Father will give you whatever you ask in my name. This
is my command: Love each other.*

John 15: 16 –17 *NIV*

The first ten years of our life together were spent in the rented downstairs of a brownstone two-family in old Chicago. Working full-time and renting didn't offer much opportunity for gardening. My husband and I discovered the town of our dreams while camping and decided to move to Rockford, ninety miles from Chicago. We were finally going to have our own home, and I was going to have my own garden.

Amid hundreds of boxes stacked everywhere, we enjoyed our first Thanksgiving dinner in our manufactured home that we shared with our faithful dachshund and two mischievous cats. Instead of finding a home for more of our belongings, after our hearty dinner we headed outdoors to rake our own leaves and plan our own gardens.

Working our way around the house to the area tucked behind the screened porch, we discovered a kidney-shaped rock garden that contained several clumps of dead plants. Immediately my horticultural impulses began working and I decided that those dried up things needed to go the way of the fallen leaves. In the spring, that would be our rose garden complete with a white arbor in the middle and the ideal burial grounds for our beloved first dog.

Before the leaf-bags were tied up, I had gingerly pulled up all these unwanted plants and began visualizing my exquisite roses.

All winter as the snow piled high over our entire property, I pored over gardening books and catalogs, drawing plans for the colors, shapes and varieties that would be needed to implement my design.

The last of the snow had hardly melted away when I began to till the soil in my rock garden. Day by day we watched the flower beds that surrounded the house come alive with all kinds of surprises. One day daffodils popped up, weeks later peonies appeared, and I continued to meticulously till and plant my rock garden. I checked to be sure I had removed, I thought, all traces of those old dead plants and made regular visits to garden shops to secure needed rose bushes within our budget. Carefully I began to plant until it looked like something out of a gardening book. To give it a finished rustic look, I spread bark chips around the bushes to cover the soil. When I finished, my neighbor, who had previously owned a farm and was definitely the neighborhood horticulturalist, came over to view the fruits of my labors. He remarked how nice the roses looked but inquired why I had removed all the former plants. In my very most professional gardening voice, I explained that they were all dead and needed to be replaced. To which he informed me that they were chrysanthemums and would have returned with the warmth of summer and bloomed again in the fall.

Stunned, I realized that a gal formerly from the South, had

a lot to learn about northern gardening, and a lot to learn about chrysanthemums.

As spring rolled into summer and the roses bloomed, little unplanned green plants kept popping up through the bark covering. Reaching in between the rose bushes to retrieve them was sometimes a painful process because many of the rose bushes had not only the biggest first-year blossoms in town, but also the biggest thorns. But I persisted until as fall was approached and, these little determined plants took over. It seemed like in a matter of weeks they emerged, grew tall and blossomed. As the roses closed their season of blooming, the chrysanthemums took center stage and put on their fall show amid the dormant roses.

For the next few years, I pampered the roses with every kind of fertilizer and method of pruning in the book but found them to be fragile and high-maintenance garden members. But the determined, dedicated chrysanthemums always appeared on schedule and fulfilled their garden duties and then quietly waited to be called upon the next season when they were needed.

Gardens, like cathedrals, need a place for their roses, but can't seem to flourish without their chrysanthemums.

***Prayer:** Lord, may we be open to your call to faithfully serve whenever and wherever needed. May we be fed by your word, watered by your love, and pruned by your correction so that we might bear fruitfully in your service.*

Rose

More than one hundred species make up the Rosa genus of the family Rosaceae. Although there is no single system of classification for garden roses, they appear to be divided into three main groups: wild roses, old garden roses and modern garden roses.

A **wild rose** is one that nature created, not one hybridized by man. There are about 100 of these basic native species of roses all having five petals. These are known to botanists as "Species Roses."

Old garden roses date back to the Roman Empire and are the predecessor of today's roses. Rose petals were used at their celebrations and is perhaps the origin of rose petals being strewn by a flower girl at today's weddings. They constitute a large variety of roses still grown today that are hardy and able to withstand winter, as well as, being suited for warm climates. They are beautiful and fragrant.

Many of the **modern garden roses** have old garden rose ancestry. The classifications of modern garden roses seems to be made by growth and flowering characteristics. The well-loved hybrid tea rose produces one large bud per stem. Although they are very popular and have produced some of the most beautiful and unusual colors, they are a high maintenance plant. One of the most loved of this group is the yellow "Peace" rose.

Other popular modern garden roses are the floribunda, which grows into a shrub with clusters of flowers, and the miniature and climbing or rambling rose.

Much symbolism has evolved from the rose. The ancient Greeks and Romans related their goddesses of love with roses. In Rome the wild rose was used to mark a room of a confidential meeting, which led to the expression "*sub rosa*" meaning to keep a secret.

The popularity of the rose is evidenced in many ways. It is the national flower for both England and the United States; four of our states— Georgia, Iowa, North Dakota and New York — have a rose for their state flower. The city of Portland, Oregon, is known as the "City of Roses" and holds an annual Rose Festival. Tyler, Texas, is known as the "Rose Capital of America" because of the large number of rose bushes they ship. Americans gather in front of their TVs every year to watching the Rose Bowl Parade and bowl game.

Most roses have prickles, not thorns as most people call them. A thorn is actually a modified leaf, but the protrusions on roses are sharp prickles which are modified epidermal stem tissue.

Roses are not raised for beauty alone. The attar, or rose oil, extracted from the rose petals is used to produce perfumes. Some of the finest attar comes from Kazanlak Valley, Bulgaria. Although there are more than seven thousand varieties of roses grown worldwide, only a few are oil producing. For more than three hundred years, the Bulgarian *Rosa Damascena*, has been grown and is considered the best oil-bearing rose. Because it takes about 60,000 roses to produce one ounce of oil, it is not surprising that today's price is about $400 an ounce.

The beauty and fragrance of the petals are usually what we think of when roses come to mind, but when they disappear, they leave behind their fruit or rose hip. The rose hip of some species, especially the Dog Rose and Cinnamon Rose, are used as a source of vitamin C. During World War II, the British gathered wild-grown rose hips to produce vitamin C syrup for the children, due to the lack of citrus fruit being imported.

Rose hips are used for herbal tea, jams, jellies, syrup, and are also great in pies. A dried and powdered form is fed to horses to improve their coats.

The rose is another example that beauty isn't just skin deep.

The Way of Love

If I speak with human eloquence and angelic ecstasy but don't love, I'm nothing but the creaking of a rusty gate.

If I speak God's Word with power, revealing all his mysteries and making everything plain as day, and if I have faith that says to a mountain, "Jump," and it jumps, but I don't love, I'm nothing.

If I give everything I own to the poor and even go to the stake to be burned as a martyr, but I don't love, I've gotten nowhere. So no matter what I say, what I believe, and what I do, I'm bankrupt without love.

Love never gives up.

Love cares more for others than for self.

Love doesn't strut,

Doesn't have a swelled head,

Doesn't force itself on others,

Isn't always "me first,"

Doesn't fly off the handle,

Doesn't keep score of the sins of others,

Doesn't revel when others grovel,

Takes pleasure in the flowering of truth,

Puts up with anything,

31

Ginger Schmidt

Trusts God always,

Always looks for the best,

Never looks back,

But keeps going to the end.

I Corinthians 13:1–7 The Message

Seeds of Faith

Great is his faithfulness; his loving kindness begins

afresh each day.

Lamentations 3:23 *LB*

> *Let us hold unswervingly to the hope we profess, for he*
> *who promised is faithful.*

> Hebrews 10:23 *NIV*

It was the last night at youth fellowship camp. The dinner bell outside the chow hall sounded calling us to evening vespers. Noisy groups of teens headed across campus for their last gathering together. I walked alone, unable to understand my own feelings as this time of study and sharing was ending. I had come to fellowship camp many times, but this time was different. As a thirteen-year old girl, I was searching for answers. Seeking to discover who I was and why I was here.

As I entered the camp chapel, a counselor was playing hymns on an old portable pump organ. In the front of the room was a homemade altar with a towering cross crafted from two gnarled wild oak limbs. The arms of the cross were covered with Spanish moss, gathered from the trees that engulfed the campground. The trailing, gray, vine-like moss as it hung downward resembled a veil and the surrounding candlelight cast an added feeling of mystery to the cross.

I was unaware of other campers as they filled the benches around me. Neither the sweltering heat of the evening nor the occasional whine of a mosquito seemed to penetrate my thoughts. What does God want me to do with my life? How do you really follow Jesus? Study groups, outdoor activities and fellowship with other teens had filled the week, each bringing joy and comfort to my confused feelings of unworthiness. Now it was the last night, and my unanswered quest seemingly was coming to an end; or so I thought.

I sat for what seemed like an eternity, listening to the music, listening to the humming of the oscillating fans used to stir the hot summer air, listening to my heart beating with an empty feeling.

I can't tell you what songs we sang or what the pastor said because it was that cross, covered with the Spanish moss, moss that lives off the trees it inhabits; moss, that clings to tree's branches with great tenacity so the wind will not blow it away; that moss, that needed the strong arms of the cross to hold onto; seemed to be calling me.

Suddenly, I realized that I didn't need to fully understand what I was to accomplish in life, or what steps I needed to take next. I just needed to hang on to *Christ,* who had died for me.

I went forward and knelt at the rough-hewn altar rail and gave my heart to Jesus.

I've strayed many times from the pathway that I pledged to follow that night, but like the Spanish moss, I've clung to the loving and forgiving arms of Christ, my Savior.

As I work in my garden, I often find a clump of Spanish moss clinging to the crepe myrtle, trying to grow strong enough to take its place on the higher branches. Daily I will return to watch it grow, reminded of the night I asked Christ to take hold of my life and help me grow.

Prayer: Loving and forgiving Father, you have promised to be with us and guide us day by day; step by step along our way. Thank you for believing in us, trusting us, guiding us. Thank you for your promise of eternal life, through your Son, Jesus.

Spanish Moss

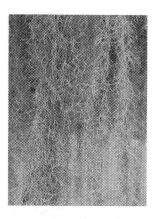

It is easy to understand how Spanish moss received its scientific name, *Tillandsia usneoides*. *Usnea* is a bearded lichen, however Spanish Moss, believed to be a lichen, is neither a moss nor a lichen, but rather a flowering plant. It is actually a bromeliad that grows hanging from tree branches. Spanish moss is an epiphyte (Greek "*epi*" upon, "phyte" plant) that lives upon other plants. Because it absorbs food from the tree and water from the air, it is known as an "air plant." It doesn't really eat the tree, but may cause damage by reducing the amount of light to the tree's leaves and increasing wind resistance during storms. It has aerial roots and tiny, inconspicuous flowers.

The plant has a slender stem with thin, curly leaves that grow like a downward hanging chain. It reproduces from seed and small fragments that are transported by the wind or are carried by birds from tree to tree.

Spanish Moss seems to prefer the live oak, bald cypress, elms, holly and pecan trees in the South. It can grow so thick that it often gives the trees a medieval appearance. Especially found throughout the South, it has become the picturesque setting for many writings and paintings.

When the French first came to Louisiana, the Native Americans called it "*Itla-okla*" or tree hair. However, the French thought that it resembled the long beards of the Spanish explorers and renamed it Spanish Moss. In Hawaii Spanish Moss is called Pele's hair, named for the Hawaiian goddess.

Not only enjoyed for its appearance, Spanish Moss has had a number of practical uses. In the mid-1900s about twelve hundred carloads of Spanish Moss were shipped for commercial use. This market was developed after the Civil War when it began being used in the stuffing for furniture. It made an ideal choice because no known insects would attack the fiber and its resilience was next only to human hair. In recent years this trade has declined due to the development of new fibers. Today the fiber is used for arts and crafts and for flower garden bedding.

As children we were warned not to play in the moss because it was home to "chiggers." However, it only collects these tiny biting mites after it has touched the ground.

The fascination that it holds for many people has been expressed in legends. One of the most popular is the ballad "Spanish Moss," composed by Canadian singer-songwriter, Gordon Lightfoot.

*No dear brothers, I am still not all I should be but
I am bringing all my energies to bear on this one
thing: Forgetting the past and looking forward to
what lies ahead, I strain to reach the end of the race
and receive the prize for which God is calling us up
to heaven because of what Christ Jesus did for us.*

Philippians 3:13–14 *LB*

Webster defines a "**weed**" as "a wild plant growing where it is not
wanted." As a child growing up in the South, I defined a weed
as a "periwinkle." They grew in vacant lots, in my mother's well-
planned gardens and they even popped up in our grass. They
grew in the broiling, hot sun, without water and survived the
monsoons of a hurricane.

Because my mother was an import from Michigan, she
possessed neither a southern accent, a love for grist or an
attachment to periwinkles.

My job was to rid the world of these unwanted garden
residents. Every Saturday before I could go fishing, I had to pull
up, by the roots, every periwinkle that had invaded our yard that
week. My attempts to point out how pretty the pink, lavender
and white blossoms were fell on deaf ears. And so I pulled them
up.

After moving to Illinois, I joined the millions of Chicagoans
that couldn't wait to flock to their neighborhood garden shop as
soon as the post-snow mud slides turned green. Searching the

budget aisle of the perennial section, my non-gardening husband placed his selection in our shopping cart. Proudly he announced that he had found some cute little pink and white flowers. When I checked out his find, I stared in utter amazement. "Periwinkles!" I exclaimed in a somewhat loud voice. But he insisted the sign said, "Vinca." I didn't care what the sign said, those were periwinkles. I should know. And I continued my speech about these useless weeds, until I discovered that he had quietly slipped away, and I was preaching to myself. Feeling badly about my lack of interest in his selection, I paid for the contents of our basket, including the periwinkles.

Once home, I began planting our spring garden beauties. When I got to the flat of vinca, (if they were going to be in our garden they had to have a different name), I chose a spot in the far corner where they might reside by themselves. As I placed each plant in the soil, I wondered what qualities they had developed to become chosen by gardeners. They were hardy, dependable, and resilient. Are these not the qualities that a employer looks for in an employee? Are these not the qualities that God looks for in us? What one gardener sees as a weed another sees as garden plant. Each plant has its own importance and needs a place to grow and develop.

Prayer: Lord, you overlook our weakness and our unfaithfulness and see only our strengths and potential. Teach us to search for and find in others the fruits you have sown in them. Help us to value each individual as a keeper in our gardens.

Periwinkle

There is much confusion over the name "periwinkle." The reason for this confusion is that two genera of the Apocynaceae or dogbane family— *Vinca* and *Catharanthus* have both acquired the common name "periwinkle."

In Chaucer's day, it was known as "parwynke" but today in various countries is known as ground ivy, cockles, pennywinkle and virginflower.

Vinca has five different species, and all have slender trailing stems that often take root, when they touch the ground causing them to spread rapidly even in places where they are not wanted. The flowers, usually violet or occasionally white, bloom most of the year.

Vinca Major is a large leaf periwinkle and used for ground cover found in southern California. It is a fire-retardant, drought-resistant and erosion-preventive plant. It will grow thick enough to prevent erosion and will choke out other grass or brush. In some areas it has been used as a grass substitute.

This flower has become so popular that 2002 was declared *The Year of the Vinca* by the National Garden Bureau.

These little plants not only provide the garden with color and disease-resistant plants, they have also obtained standing with the pharmaceutical industry. The alkaloids vincristine and vinblastine contained in the sap, although poisonous if ingested, have become an effective treatment for leukemia and lymphoma. In its native land of Madagascar, they have been used as an herbal medicine to treat diabetes, bleeding disorders, tranquilizers and disinfectants.

A close relative, *Catharanthus* closely resembles *Vinca Minor* and was first named *C. rosea* meaning rose-colored. Because rosea is feminine it was later changed to *C. roseus,* masculine to match the genus name *Cartharanthus,* meaning pure flower.

Both *vinca* and *C. roseaus* are single flowers with overlapping petals. However the *C. roseus* is white or rosy pink with a small mauve "eye" in the center.

All throughout Florida and other areas of the South, these plants were the wild flower occupants of vacant lots and rarely coveted for gardens. Today they are usually purchased in your local garden shop and are well worth the investment in your garden. But once started, you'll find them difficult to control.

The person who does the planting or watering isn't very important, but God is important because he is the one who makes things grow.

I Corinthians 3: 7 LB

Hurrying to the "Slop Shop" where the student mailboxes were housed, I joined the hoard of students all rushing to retrieve their mail. A letter with some cash, a box of cookies from home, almost anything brought joy to the heart of a college student away from home.

Smashed against the wall of boxes, I finally got mine open, and pulled out a rather fat oversized brown envelope addressed in my mother's beautiful handwriting. Finding it too fat for money, too small for something new to wear, curiosity overwhelmed me. I finally squeezed my way through the crowd and headed for my dorm. Rapidly ripping open the envelope, I extracted its contents. Unwrapping layer after layer of tissue paper and arriving at a plastic bag, I beheld a leaf, a large, fat, green leaf. The note that accompanied this curious item read: "I know you miss our gardens, so pin this on your curtain and watch it grow."

Great, just what I needed, I thought. Five dollars would have been most useful, but a green leaf for my curtain was somewhat unwelcomed. I suddenly remembered that Mother had these leaves pinned to the sunroom curtains and I'd hear her talk to them, complimenting them on their daily growth. Feeling sure it would make her happy, I reluctantly found a straight pin, attached it to our drapes and admonished it to do its thing and grow.

Days went by, weeks went by, and I completely forgot about the leaf. But without my verbal encouragements, it had been doing its thing – growing. It wasn't until my roommate asked what that awful stuff was growing all over the drapes that I gave it another thought. Out of tiny crevasses around the outer edge of the leaf miniature plants were growing. New life from a plain old leaf. No soil, no water, no tender loving care, I didn't even talk to it as Mother did. It just had a job to do and day in and day out went about the task of hanging on to a piece of fabric for dear life, growing and producing new little plants.

Suddenly the overwhelming life of a freshman college student with its new environment – dorm life, making new friends, sixteen hours of classes, thirty-two plus hours studying; extra-curricular activities and even the cafeteria food – didn't seem so impossible.

Perhaps I had forgotten to hang on to the promise that *I can do all things through him* who strengthens me. (Philippians 4:13).

Prayer: Father, remind us that your plans for our lives are complete in every detail, and to fulfill them all we have to do is have faith, trust in You and obey Your word.

Kalanchoe pinnata

Kalanchoe pinnata, sometimes called Miracle Leaf, Cathedral Bells, Goethe Plant and Katakataka, is a succulent plant native to Madagascar belonging to genus, *Kalanchoe.*

It's not difficult to see why some call this plant "Miracle Leaf" because small plantlets grow from the fringes of the leaves even when the leaves has been detached from the plant. They drop off and root, forming many new plants in a single location. Because of this rapid growth in many areas, they are considered an invasive species.

One of its common names, Goethe Plant, was a result of the great interest that Johann Wolfgang von Goethe, a writer and amateur gardener, had in this plant. He raised them and often gave them as gifts to people who visited his home.

The plant produces bell-shaped blossoms that dangle downward in clusters separating them from other Kalanchoe plants, but accounting for the common name, Cathedral bells. My mom called her plants church bells. Why, I'll never know, but perhaps because we never worshiped at a cathedral.

The leaves are reported to be poisonous especially to animals, having a cardiac effect of slowing the heart rate. Folklore records that material pounded from the leaves has been used as a poultice for sprains, infections and burns.

For many years these leaves were popular Florida souvenirs. Sealed in a small cellophane (before the days of plastics) bag, and a postcard attached with instructions on how to hang them up and watch them grow, they were mailed to friends back home. Because they sometimes began to sprout in route, I'm sure they weren't popular with the mailman.

Today due to the overdevelopment of some areas of Florida, they are difficult to locate.

But He was wounded for our transgressions, crushed
for our iniquities; upon him punishment that made us
whole, and by his bruises we are healed.

Isaiah 53:5 *NRSV*

In 1936, we moved from Michigan to Florida for my mother's health. Three years later, my dad spent his winter shore leave building us a modest home on a small lot, in the tiny Florida town we would call home for many decades.

When spring came and the Great Lakes were navigable, my dad was called back to his ship. A sad six-year-old bid good-bye to her dad, and my mother began her year-long complaining that the house was not quite finished. The unfinished part—the front portico. It seems that she had planted a passion vine in position to start its climb up the trellis that was to be the covering for the front doorway and now it had nothing to climb up. However, when dad got his call, he had 24-hours to report to his ship; his company and crew did not understand that he hadn't built mother's trellis.

During that spring, summer and fall, mother carefully watered and tended this tiny vine. When dad arrived the following winter, we hardly had the Christmas presents opened when he was assigned the duty of trellis building. When it was finished, it really made our house a beautiful home. What was more important, it provided mother's passion vine with a perfect dwelling.

Year after year, the vine grew until it had climbed up, over and down the entire trellis. The flowers were beautiful and the delicate fragrance was a perfect greeting to guests.

During the next awful war years, it provided table decorations for our church's Lenten dinners, and mother even developed her own recipe for passion fruit jelly.

The Atlantic hurricane season is from June 1 to November 30. However, when we make it to September, we begin to feel that we are on the homeward stretch. The Ft. Lauderdale hurricane of 1947 (they started naming the hurricanes in 1950) was a whopper. It was a category four hurricane, packing winds of one hundred and sixty miles per hour. It swept through our area on September 17th, taking with it our front portico and mother's passion vine.

When the storm subsided, the neighborhood came alive with its grateful inhabitants investigating their damage. Mother's passion vine appeared to have left the area with our front portico and was nowhere to be found.

Dad got off the ship and flew home to help assess the damage and rebuild the front of the house. It was then that we noticed, peeking out of the dirt next to the porch, sprouts and green leaves. The plant was alive and growing again.

Surprising, amazing, unbelievable? Not really. After all, it was a passion vine which Christians for centuries believed contained many prophetic symbols.

This unusual plant was often used as a visual means of teaching the Gospel story of Christ's passion to people who had no printed Bibles. The story explained that the spiraled **tendrils** hanging from the vine represented the whips used in the scourging of Christ, and the pointed tips of the **leaves** were likened to the head of the Centurion's spear used to pierce his side.

The **central column** of the flower was symbolic of the pillar used for Christ's scourging and the **chalice-shaped ovary** with its receptacle, as the cup of the Last Supper. It was also told that the seventy two **radial filaments** which tradition records were the number of thorns in the crown of thorns placed on Christ's head; the **three stigmata** represent the three nails and below them the **five anthers** the five wounds inflicted into Christ. The rounded **style** is believed to represent the sponge used to moisten Christ's lips with vinegar. Near the base if the column is a yellow ring with five spots of red that represent drops of blood from the five wounds received by our Lord.

The sweet **fragrance** is a reminder of the spices prepared by the women to anoint Christ's body and the round **fruit** that the vine produces is a symbol of the world Christ came to save.

Whether you search this unusually lovely plant for all of its Christian symbols or simply view it for its beauty, it provides a reminder that God's faithful love for us is displayed in all creation.

Prayer: *Let us not forget that you have created all things, and are in all things and have given them to us as a reminder of your love for us. Help us to see beauty and meaning in each of your creations.*

Passion Flower Vine

There are about five hundred species of flowering plants all belonging to the *Passiflora* genus of the *Passifloraceae* family. They are mostly vines with a few shrubs.

Found in many parts of the world including South America, China and Southern Asia, there are nine species that are grow in the United States from Florida to Ohio and west to California.

Because of their unique flower structure, it takes a large bee for effective pollination. Some species are pollinated by hummingbirds, bumble bees or wasps and others are self-pollinated.

While most species are an important source of nectar for many insects and the leaves food for the larva of some caterpillars, the plant seems to have a number of built-in protective measures. To prevent butterflies from laying too many eggs on a single plant, some have small colored nubs that look like the butterfly's eggs.

Thinking that the plant already has enough, the butterfly goes elsewhere. Some produce a sweet nutrient-rich liquid on their leaf stems that attracts ants which kill and eat many other pests.

Although most flowers only last one day, gardeners grow the passion flower for its beauty. However, the passion fruit or *maracujá* , which is usually round or elongated, is edible and is highly cultivated in the Caribbean, South Florida, and South Africa. It is used for juice. Maypop (*P. incarnata*) is a common species that can endure cold down to a minus four degrees and therefore is found in the north. Its sweet, yellowish fruit is about the size of an egg.

The fresh or dried leaves of the Maypop were used by North American Natives and later adapted by the colonists as a tea for the treatment of insomnia, hysteria, epilepsy and as a painkiller.

The flower is probably best known for its Christian symbolism which has stood the test of time. The origin of this story dates back to 1610, when a Mexican Augustinian friar, Emmanuel de Villegas, reported it with sketches to Jacomo Bosio, a monastic scholar who was working on his treatise on the Cross of Calvary. After much investigation to determine that the flower did exist, he presented the story to the world.

> *A very large crowd spread their cloaks on the road, while others cut branches from the trees and spread them on the road. The crowds that went ahead of him and those that followed shouted: Hosanna to the Son of David! Blessed is the one who comes in the name of the Lord! Hosanna in the highest.*

Matthew 21: 8-9 *NIV*

It was Palm Sunday and I was in charge of the children carrying palms. Traditionally our church celebrated this Holy Day with a procession into the church. First the children entered, carrying the palm branches and forming an arch for the children's choir, bell choir and then the adult choir. The minister and liturgist completed the procession.

Because a large variety of palm trees grew in the south part of Florida, it was not difficult to select just the right size and shape to do the job. This year we had switched from the small Australian cycad branches easily carried by the children with one hand, to the two-handed sago palm branches which offered a higher and fuller archway.

Once the procession was completed and while the congregation sang the last verse of "All Glory Laud and Honor," the palm-carriers placed their branches down the aisles next to the pews.

This usually went off without a hitch; however, the larger sago palm branches, in addition to being more difficult for the children to carry, also bore an uninvited guest. I couldn't believe my eyes as I watch a long green string descend from one of the palms just as the minister passed under its archway. It couldn't be, I mused. But as it began to twist and turn, I realized it was – a snake!

Before I had an opportunity to decide what to do, the children began laying their palms down the aisle and that palm ended up almost next to my pew. Throughout the entire service, I didn't take my eyes off that palm branch, or so I thought. However, as we joyously processed from the church, I spotted our uninvited guest sunning itself in the gutter of one of the sliding glass doors that formed one side of the church. It appeared completely oblivious of the significance of the occasion. Not wanting it to remain in the church, I notified a brave usher who promptly relocated our unseen guest to its more familiar surroundings outdoors.

How often is Jesus an unseen guest in our homes, our churches, and our hearts? How often does he come to us and we don't feel his presence; yet He stays and continues to love us. Everyone in the church that day was too busy, too excited, too occupied to notice one of God's creatures. And yet amid all the activity of the day, it stayed.

Prayer: Forgive us when we treat Jesus like an unseen guest, our when we fail to recognize the new worshiper in our midst. Help us to remember Christ's words that when we have shared with one of the least of his brethren, we have shared with him.

Ginger Schmidt

Palm Trees and Cycads

Although often confused by newcomers and natives alike, palm trees and cycads are not related.

Palm trees belong to the *Arecaceae* family of flowering plants. There are about twenty six hundred species, most of which live in the tropics, subtropics and warm temperate climates. They have large, compound, evergreen leaves arranged at the top of an unbranched stem, making some of them resemble a concrete post with feathers. Palms may also grow in clusters, putting up new shoots from the base.

One of the most photographed palms is *Cocos* or the coconut palm, whose trunk can make an almost ninety degree curve, and produce the coveted coconut that cooks sprinkle on many tropical dishes. The *Roystonea regia*, royal palm, which stands fifty to one hundred feet tall and can grow at a rate of a foot a year, is often used to ornamentally line streets. A good example of this is the famous Royal Palm Way in Palm Beach. Most palm trees are extremely resistant to salt spray and high winds and during a hurricane can be observed swaying and bending with the wind, but coming through without a scratch.

Palm trees are mentioned thirty times in the Bible and in many cultures they symbolize victory, peace and fertility. The Romans rewarded champions of games and military heroes with palm branches, early Christians used the palm branch to symbolize victory of the faithful over enemies of the soul. It is still used in many countries in the Palm Sunday celebrations. The palm appears on clothing, pottery and even on the South Carolina flag. That state is known as the Palmetto State after the Cabbage Palmetto. During the Revolutionary War, palmetto logs, because of their spongy wood which would absorb the British cannonballs, were used to build Fort Moultrie.

Palms are not just something to view, but are important for palm oil, a vegetable cooking oil; dates from the date palm; coir, a course, water-resistant fiber from the outer shell of coconuts for door mats; and the milk and meat of the coconut as a food. Even the sago palm provides starch made from the pith of the trunk.

A few palms have become threatened by human intervention. Many trees have been lost during the over-development of land. The harvesting the heart of palms, a popular vegetable used in salads, removes the inner core of the certain palms and kills the plant. At least one hundred species are currently endangered and nine species are reported extinct.

Cycads are a group of seed plants having a large crown of compound leaves and a stout trunk. An inhabitant of the tropical and subtropical climates as well as Japan, China and Southeast Asia, they are often mistaken for ferns or palms but really belong to the order *Cycadales.*

There are more than three hundred species. Tribal people used the stems to produce a starch and the nuts which they used as food. However, great care had to be taken to soak the nuts enough to remove the nerve toxin which they contain.

Cycads are used for landscaping because they do not need a lot of tender loving care. They grow in almost any medium and do not require a lot of water.

The grass withers and the flowers fall, but the word of God stands forever.

Isaiah 40:8 *NIV*

School teacher, college admissions counselor, receptionist had been some of my titles, but private secretary was a new assignment. However, with great excitement and a little trepidation, I began my duties as secretary to the Provincial Superior of the Sisters of Resurrection in Chicago.

I soon realized that this was not a "job," but a "calling, a privilege to serve."

My office was not in the hospital that the sisters sponsored, but in the convent across the street that was their home. And I soon felt like part of their family, serving with the sisters and not an employee toiling at a desk.

The convent was almost a century old and in the early days had been home to both the sisters and the residential students whom they taught. It was rich in history and lovely in architecture.

When I began my work, the ground was covered with Chicago snow and ice that within a few short months gave way to a carpet of lush green grass and trees bursting with fresh spring leaves. There stood one tree still barren of leaves directly in front of the convent. Then, without any warning, it was suddenly covered with big, fuzzy buds, but still no leaves. Entering the driveway one morning, I noticed that the tree had turned a delicate shade of pink.

As I passed sisters in the hallway, each one gave a cherry greeting and asked if I had seen the magnolias. Puzzled I asked, "what magnolias?" In answer to my question, I was ushered into the library. There, framed by an old, Gothic window, was that strangely beautiful tree. Having come from the South where magnolia trees have huge white elegant blossoms, I questioned the accuracy of their scientific classification. However there was no doubt that the sight that was unfolding before me was, in its own way, as beautiful as the magnificent magnolias of my childhood. Every day I visited the window for this special view and sadly watched as the weeklong drama unfolded and then vanished leaving behind an umbrella of green leaves.

I soon discovered that the deciduous (northern) *magnolia x soulagiana*, was a saucer magnolia related to our evergreen (southern) *magnolia grandiflora* whose beauty I had fallen in love with many years ago.

I could easily share the sisters' excitement to witness this tree shed its drab winter garb and put on a fresh new outfit for spring. It was almost as awesome as my first encounter with the magnificent white *grandiflora* of the South.

Transferred from the southeast coast of Florida to the north central part of the state for the second phase of my education, I, a weary freshman, longed for the rigors of the classroom to end. I didn't think anything could lift my spirits as I crossed the campus that morning. The birds sounded so happy, why didn't I? Then I noticed that the trees that dotted the grounds were suddenly decorated with huge white blossoms. Their delicate fragrance was a lot more inviting than our breakfast at the commons. They were huge, the biggest flowers I'd ever seen. Not wanting to admit that I couldn't immediately identify them, I made a note to check them out in the library later that day. Thumbing through a southern plant guide, I spied it—"Magnolia, any tree or shrub of the genus *Magnolia*, cultivated for its dark-green foliage and large wax-like flowers in the spring." Magnolia, I even liked the sound of the word as it rolled off my lips.

For the next couple of weeks until the blossoms disappeared I couldn't get enough viewing time. I made it my mission to go from point "A" to point "B" by way of one of the trees, drinking in its fragrance.

The next spring, I kept a watchful eye so I wouldn't miss a moment of their arrival. That was when our great love affair began. First noticing the tan buds that appeared at the tip of a branch, I watched daily as they grew in size until the sheath of protective covering parted, giving birth to its occupant. Almost before my eyes, I could see the huge waxy-white petals open and spread their arms out to bathe in the sunshine. It seemed a shame that this beauty couldn't last forever. But it soon began to fade as the petals aged and departed, leaving behind the cone-like fruit which, as it enlarged and turned red, enhanced the tree with a new beauty. Then they split open and shared their seeds with hungry birds and squirrels and perhaps gave birth to a new tree nearby. The splendor of this tree always brought a feeling of new life to me as I watched this parade of life unfold. For centuries in the language of flowers, Magnolias have stood for nobility, dignity and perseverance — for me they stood for the promise of eternal life.

Prayer: *Father, You have shared with us the beauty of the earth as a witness of your everlasting love for us. Strengthen our faith in the knowledge that as our years fade away you have provided us with the gift of eternal life through the sacrifice of your son, Jesus Christ.*

Magnolia

More than two hundred species belong to the Magnoliaceae family. They are found in parts of Asia; North, South and Central America and the West Indies.

This flowering tree, originally known as talauma, was discovered on the island of Martinique in 1703 by Charles Plumier. He named it in honor of a French botanist, Pierre Magnol.

Magnolia grandiflora or southern magnolia and *Magnolia x soulagiana* or saucer magnolia will be explored here.

Magnolia x soulagiana is both a large shrub and deciduous tree which will grow up to thirty feet in height and in cold climates is one of the first trees to bloom in the spring. Its blossoms range from deep purple to light pink and some are pure white. Each flower has six waxy petals first shaped like a goblet and when completely open it forms a saucer. For a brief week or more the tree is completely covered with blossoms, and with no leaves having appeared, it creates a spectacular sight.

The Magnolia grandiflora is an evergreen tree that keeps a healthy covering of large shiny, deep-green leaves year round. These are found mostly in the milder climate of southeastern United States. They bud in late March or early April and by mid-June they have put forth their enormous white, waxy blossoms which maintain their beauty for only a day or two. The blossom, which sometimes reaches almost a foot in diameter, consists of six to twelve petals that open to reveal the greenish-gold colored carpel, the female parts. At the base of the carpel are rings of purple pollen-bearing stamens. This centerpiece stands in contrast to the white petals to create the beauty of this showy flower. As the petals brown and drop off, the cone-shaped fruit appears and changes color until it becomes a deep red, remaining on the tree until early fall when it pops open revealing its bright red seeds.

Although basically enjoyed as an ornamental tree, the bark from some magnolia trees has been used as a traditional medicine in China known as *hou po*. This bark has been shown to reduce allergic and asthmatic reactions.

Because magnolia trees are so abundant in the state of Mississippi, it has become known as the "Magnolia State" and is the official state flower and tree.

> **"I tell you the truth, if you have faith as small as a mustard seed, you can say to this mountain, move from here to there and it will move. Nothing will be impossible for you."**

Matthew 17:20 NIV

During the days after my husband's death, the snow, sleet and bitter winds were relentless. My decision to return to my native state and family, the endless packing, and the thought of leaving the little home that we had loved and shared was becoming overwhelming. For days, I had noticed a strange plant that had pushed its way out of a crack in the sidewalk beneath my snow-covered bird feeder. I watched in amazement as it made its way through the snow and up the side of the garage in search of sunlight and warmth. *That's a tough little weed* I had thought and dismissed it tenacity from my mind.

I had spent the morning carefully packing our collection of wood-carved animals and awards for my husband's outstanding work as an outdoor writer. Occasionally I stopped to tend a large pot of my famous pea soup cooking on the stove and the bread baking in the oven. My heart was heavy as I gathered up the last contributions I would be sharing with friends at my church's Lenten luncheon.

As I stepped out the front door, soup pot in hand, my eyes were drawn to the hearty plant that was determined to survive the bitter winter we were experiencing. But to my surprise the tall stem and green leaves were topped by a huge yellow flower that nodded its head as it was whipped by the wind. What I thought was a weed was not a weed at all, but a beautiful sunflower.

I stood for a breathless moment staring at this amazing blossom that dared to brave such a cold and barren place to reach upward and share its beauty with me. It was certainly a living example of a bumper sticker that I had stuck on my car many years ago that read, "Bloom Where Planted."

Surely, I thought, if this small seed could find enough nourishment to germinate and push its way up through a crack in the cement, enduring the cold of winter to share its beauty with me, I could be transplanted to a new community and bloom where planted.

Prayer: *Father, help us to take that small seed of faith that you plant in us and nourish it and cultivate it so that it will grow stronger each day. Give us faith to withstand the bumps in the road and continue our journey to the end.*

Sunflower

The sunflower is the state flower of Kansas, and a favorite decoration on almost everything from dishes to T-shirts.

Helianthus annuus, more commonly known as the sunflower is a sturdy plant that can reach eight to ten feet tall and produce a head or composite flower almost a foot in diameter.

The head is made up of the outer or sterile ray of florets that are usually yellow, but can be maroon, orange and other colors. The florets inside the circular head, called the disc florets, mature into the fruit or sunflower seeds.

The inner florets which are arranged in a spiraling pattern produce a unique and complicated mathematical arrangement.

Sunflower buds display heliotropism, the directional growth of a plant in relation to sunshine. Sunrise finds them facing east and slowly during the day they follow the sun and by evening are facing west. This process ends when the bud opens into a flower that remains frozen facing east. When growing in the wild, only the leaves display this movement, switching from east to west like the arms of a dancer.

The sunflower appears to be native to the Americas. Domesticated first in Mexico, it may have been introduced to the Mississippi Valley as early as 2000 B.C. Many natives used the sunflower as a symbol of the sun god. During the eighteenth century, sunflower oil became very popular in Europe because it was one of the few oils permitted by the Russian Orthodox Church during Lent.

Today sunflower whole seed is roasted and sold as snack food. It is also used as an alternative to peanut butter and in Germany is mixed with rye flour to make "Sonnenblumenkernbrot" bread. Every part of the sunflower seed can be used. After the oil has been extracted for cooking oils, the cake-like remains are used for livestock feed. However, farmers growing various crops still consider the sunflower a nuisance especially in the Midwest where they have a negative effect on the corn and soybean production.

When someone becomes a Christian he becomes a brand new person inside. He is not the same any more. A new life has begun!

II Corinthians 5:17 *LB*

Following my husband's death, I moved back to my home state of Florida and purchased a mobile home that obviously had been owned by a non-gardener. The entire yard was void of anything blooming. While there was much work to do inside, the yard kept beckoning to me. After making a drawing of my planned landscaping, I headed to the garden shop to purchase as many plants as my budget would allow.

A display of caladium bulbs caught my eye and for a very small amount of money, I knew the colorful heart-shaped leaves would provide great beauty. Into an empty flat container, I carefully placed my selections, separating them by color, size and shape and marking each section so I could later arrange them to fit my pattern.

Once home, I hurried to my new garden area with my bulbs and my garden tools. But in my haste, I tripped over a hidden sprinkler head, spilling my bulbs across the grass and thus ending my careful planning.

One by one I picked up each bulb, dumped it into my carrier and marched forward to the garden area determined to still create something. Digging little holes to form a border, I dropped into the rich earth a small brown bulb, pondering the wonderment of how it would soon open up into a beautiful cluster of colorful leaves. Each bulb appeared the same. Because I could no longer tell one from another, I didn't know which one would turn out to be a delicate green and white lacey design or which one would burst into a profusion of reds to accent its deep green background. But each bulb had the potential to produce great beauty. Patting the earth over them, I knew that in a few short months the shoots would break ground and they would gradually push their way upward, unfolding to display their unique characteristics. Each would be lovely in its own way and would contribute to the beauty of the garden. Daily I watered them and waited.

As the tip of each leaf broke through the soil and began its journey upward it began to unfold until it revealed its ordained design. The leaf started out small and then gradually grew in size and depth of color. Each bulb produced not one but numerous leaves, each uniquely beautiful. They produced an artistic border crafted far more lovely than anything I could have planned. I was certainly not a Master Gardener, but I knew who was.

Prayer: God, thank you for the new life you have planted in each of us. Help us to cultivate those seeds recognizing that you have given each of us uniquely different abilities to grow and blossom with your love and tender care.

Caladium

Caladiums are tropical plants belonging to the *Araceae* family and also commonly known as elephant ears, angel wings and heart of Jesus. There are more than one thousand varieties of Caladiums that originated in South America. This genus includes seven species coming from South and Central America that grow to be quite large in open areas of the forest or along waterways.

Some of these colorful leaves are cultivated especially for houseplants; although they resemble the colorful coleus, they are unrelated. They grow from corms (the underground swollen stem base of the plant) and can be divided into several plants. When grown in temperate areas they should be removed from the ground before the frost, then dried and stored. In warmer tropical temperatures they remain in the ground year round and reappear in late spring and remain colorful until early fall.

Ninety-eight percent of the bulbs are grown in Lake Placid, Florida, the *"Caladium Capital of the World."* An annual Caladium

Festival is held in this city every August to celebrate the height of the harvest. Vendors line the streets with various handmade crafts, and under huge tents at the end of the street, caladium growers display the newest and best of their year's crops. Garden enthusiasts stand in line to purchase their selections. While extremely beautiful as decorator plants, they are quite toxic to children and pets.

The Who, What When, Why and How of Faith…

Who…

You can never please God without faith, without depending on him. Anyone who wants to come to God must believe that there is a God and that he rewards those who sincerely look for him.

Hebrews 11:6 *LB*

What…

The fundamental fact of existence is that this trust in God, this faith, is the firm foundation under everything that makes life worth living. It's our handle on what we can't see. The act of faith is what distinguished our ancestors, set them above the crowd.

Hebrews 11: 6 The Message

When…

The steadfast love of the Lord never ceases,

His mercies never come to an end;

They are new every morning;

Great is your faithfulness.

Lamentations 3:22-23 *NRSV*

Why...

> *For by grace you have been saved through faith, and this*
> *is not your own doing; it is a gift of God.*

> Ephesians 2:8–10 NRSV

How...

> *Therefore we do not lose heart. Though outwardly we*
> *are wasting away, yet inwardly we are being renewed*
> *day by day. For our light and momentary troubles are*
> *achieving for us an eternal glory that far outweighs them*
> *all. So we fix our eyes not on what is seen, but on what*
> *is unseen. For what is seen in temporary, but what is*
> *unseen is eternal.*

> II Corinthians 4:16-18 *NIV*

Love puts fuel in our tanks to get us going, but faith keep us on the journey.

There would be no faith, if there were no bumps along the journey.

Seeds of Patience

...being strengthened with all power according to his glorious might so that you may have great endurance and patience...

Colossians 1: 11 NIV

Although the Lord gives you the bread of adversity and the water of affliction, your teachers will be hidden no more; with your own eyes you will see them.

Isaiah 30:20 *NIV*

Little girls want to do things for their parents to say, I love you. At school we made cards, molded our hands in plaster-of-Paris and painted pictures. But for me it was flowers. I wanted to bring home flowers to say, "I love you."

The vacant lot across the street from our house was overgrown with all sorts of shrubs, vines, and cacti, and it seemed to be luring me to explore it.

I would come home and tell my mother what new beautiful plants I had discovered and occasionally bring home some botanical wonder from my explorations. Each time that we found a container for these offerings, mother gave her commander-in-chief's warning — Don't touch that cactus! And each time I assured her that I wouldn't.

But on each expedition to my secret garden, I was attracted to the beautiful yellow flowers of the prickly pear cactus. I studied how they were situated among the sharp spines that stood out all over the big flat ear-like pads of the cactus. Calculating that there was at least a finger's width between each large thorn, I decided that with the proper tools a flower could be retrieved.

So one hot summer day, armed with a pair of pliers, a linoleum cutter from my dad's workshop and a shoebox to carry it home in, I headed out to conquer the prickly pear cactus.

I carefully sized it up, pried my little fingers in between thorns, and then I grabbed it gently with the pliers and inserted the cutter. With one swoop and a little sawing motion, I dislodged the flower from its throne and dropped it into the box. It was then that I knew why I had been warned, even commanded, to leave the cactus alone. I immediately felt the terrible painful stinging all over my fingers, back of my hand and even on my wrist. I stared at my hand, but could see nothing. I hadn't received a single thorn or so I thought. Could it be poison that the plant stored to keep away predators like me? Whatever the cause, I was doomed to hurry home and confess my sin.

Once inside the house the thrill of my conquest was gone, as I tearfully held out the shoebox in one hand and the other damaged hand.

One look and Mother knew. Why is it that mother's are like that? I could feel the lecture coming. Why is it that mother's are like that? But not this time. She took the shoebox, laid it down, and taking out her magnifying glass to examine my poor painful hand, she announced with great authority, "Young lady, your hand is covered with tiny hair-like spines." And then came the terrifying continuation, "I don't know what to do!"

Mother always knew what to do, but she had just confessed that she didn't. So I was dragged across the street to our native-Floridian neighbor who assured us she'd have them out in a jiffy.

And quicker than I could get out ten more sobs, she returned with an old white candle and some matches. Neither of these tools sparked my enthusiasm about the prospective treatment.

She lit the candle and patiently dropped the melted wax on my hand until she had a small area covered. We waited a few minutes until it hardened and she then pull it away. Bingo! It was covered with tiny almost invisible hairs that had once pierced my hand. For probably an hour, she patiently continued until the treatment ended and so did the pain.

When we returned home, Mother carefully slid the beautiful cactus flower into a bowl of water and let it float around adorning our dinner table for several days until it was given a proper burial.

Did I learn my lesson? Well, I certainly never tried to pick the blossoms of the prickly pear cactus or any other cactus again. But shamefully it wasn't the last time that I was to try my mother's patience. Now that I'm a mother, grandmother and great-grandmother I recall my mother's frequent statement that I was going to be the death of her. And it is a small wonder that I wasn't.

Prayer: Lord, teach us to listen to your instruction. Give us wisdom to know when to speak and patience to understand the impetuousness of your children.

Prickly Pear Cactus

Tall and stately, the prickly pear cactus has about a dozen species of the *Opuntia* genus of the *Cactaceae* family. These cacti have large, fleshy, flat pads which some people call leaves, but they are really the branches or stems of the plant and serve as a water reservoir for the plant. In addition to the regular large sharp spines that project from many cacti, the prickly pears have tiny, fine barbed spines called glochids. They are found in clusters above the regular spines. They are difficult to see and more difficult to remove. Believe me on that one.

Most prickly pear cacti have yellow, red or purple flowers. The different species vary in height from less than a foot to seven feet tall. Although many are found growing wild in open fields throughout the southern United States, they are grown as a food crop in many areas of the world.

They are well-suited for arid and semi-arid lands because they efficiently convert water into biomass, making them an important agricultural crop. The large, sweet fruits, called tunas, appear in early May through early summer and ripen from August through October. After removing the thick outer covering, the fruit is chilled and eaten, tasting much like watermelon. They are also used to make jams and jellies. In areas of Sicily, wine is made from the fruit.

The fruit is not the only part of the cactus which is eaten. The nopales are a coveted vegetable that come from the cladophylls or pads of the prickly pear cactus. They can be found in the vegetable section of most Hispanic grocery stores. Carefully peeled to remove the spines, they are used to prepare several commonly eaten Mexican dishes such as "tacos de nopales" or fried with jalapenos and eggs for breakfast. They are rich in fiber, vitamins and minerals.

Because the cacti grow on their own, the cattle industry of Southwest United States has used them as both a feed and water source for their cattle and as boundary fences. When a certain area of cacti is ready for feed, a worker precedes the cattle with a portable blow torch, searing off the spines. Following the feeding the cacti are left to grow more pads

Like its western cousins, in Florida the *Opuntia humifusa* is the species usually found in fields covered with scrub growth everywhere. It produces a showy yellow flower that blossoms from May to July. The fruit is round and a reddish-purple.

The biggest difference that I have noted in the prickly pear

Cactus found in Florida are those sneaky little hair-like spines that accompany the noticeable large spines.

In addition to the common usage of this cactus, Florida homeowners have adapted them to burglar-proof window areas. Planted beneath a bedroom window, no one wants to enter.

But we also rejoice in our suffering, because we know that suffering produced perseverance; perseverance, character and character hope. And hope does not disappoint us because God has poured out his love into our hearts by the Holy Spirit who he has given us.

Romans 5: 3–5 *NIV*

I was watering a few new plants that I had added to my backyard garden, when I noticed a tiny snail working its way up the bird bath. Laboriously it moved upward using a "spit and slide" motion and leaving behind a moist trail. Finally reaching the summit, it toppled into the water and, I thought, I could hear a refreshing *"ah"* as it found relief from the sweltering heat. I turned my empty dirt bucket over and sat down to observe a second one making the same journey. Watching the slow but steady parade of several snails as they conquered the great height of the bird bath in order to obtain the reward of a cool splash, I was taken back to my first Sunday at college. Our church was about a mile away from campus. The upper class students from our church met the freshmen at the campus Christian Ed building for the trip to our first fellowship gathering.

As we strolled down the tree-lined main street of town our pace kept cadence with our conversations.

Suddenly I noticed that Bill began to lag behind. Born with spina bifida, he was only able to walk using forearm crutches which he placed in front of him and dragged forward both legs. His pace was slow but steady. His face was unflinching and joyous.

I dropped back to walk with him. Articulate, humorous, polite and unwavering in his determination to be part of the group, he was a fun-loving pre-law student and fraternity man. I was a scared, insecure freshman and sorority pledge.

For the next three years, I was privileged to spend time studying together and attending many social functions with Bill.

For many occasions, he provided a terrifyingly wonderful ride in his hand-controlled car or escorted me, on foot, across campus or to church. On one of our treks to town, I asked him why he walked all the way to church. As soon as I'd ask, I knew the answer that was coming, "To get there, of course," he replied with great glee. His enthusiasm for life was contagious and was reflected in all he did.

At parties we participated in every contest, from bobbing for apples to the egg toss. And we did our share of winning, I might add.

Never complaining, always smiling, he taught me what was truly important about campus life. He may have been physically challenged, but he was not spiritually challenged. He was everybody's friend. He shared his joy for life and his commitment to Christ with all of us.

When Bill graduated and headed for law school, I missed his presence on campus, but knowing Bill had taught me how God gives each of us special gifts. For Bill it was his faith and perseverance.

Prayer: *Father, remind us that you abide with each of us through every struggle both great and small. Give us the strength and perseverance needed to joyously face our daily challenges.*

Snail

Helix aspersa, is a gastropod mollusk with a shell, simply known as the land snail. It is one of the tiniest creatures in the garden.

Less than a millimeter in size, it is able to move its coiled-shell covered body at the amazing speed of about 0.03 mph. It moves by strong rhythmic contractions of its muscular foot as it glides along on a mucus secretion which it produces to reduce friction and protect it from sharp objects.

Most snails have two pairs of tentacles on their heads. The upper set is eye stalks and the lower set provides their sense of smell. Because they don't see well, they rely on their sense of smell to locate their food.

Aquatic snails breathe using gills, while land snails have a pulmonary sac or lung in their cavity.

Land snails are hermaphrodites, having both male and female sex organs. They may lay as many as one hundred eggs which they bury in shallow soil during warm, damp weather as often as once a month. In two to four weeks the eggs will hatch.

Their slowness has become their claim to fame. We often use expressions: "a snail's pace" or "slower than a snail." With the introduction of email, our land postal system has become known as "snail mail."

Escargot is not a regular on our dinner menu, but for many it is a delicacy. Not all snails are edible, but *Helix pomatia and Helix aspersa* are species most often eaten. Because a snail's diet consists mostly of decayed matter and has to be purified before eaten, farm-raised snails that eat special diets are used for escargot.

> *My eyes stay open through the watches of the night, that I may meditate on your promises.*

> Psalm119: 148 *NIV*

Aroused from my sleep about midnight by my dad's announcement that the light show was just beginning, I headed to the pilot house with the excitement and wild anticipation of an astronomy student about to discover a new star.

Together we climbed the ladder to the top of the pilot house and huddled for hours in the last life raft to be launched in case of a disaster at sea. The early morning air was cold and Dad had thoughtfully brought an old scratchy navy blanket to keep us warm.

My summer vacations as the skipper's daughter aboard a Great Lakes freighter were coming to an end. In the fall I would start college and future summers would have to be spent working. So we were determined to cram a lifetime at sea into one last summer.

Lying on our backs and staring at the heavens, we spent the remainder of the night and into the early morning darkness watching the heavens change colors as Lake Superior was invaded by the *aurora borealis,* better known as the "northern lights."

As the colors swirled, swayed and exploded, I asked, "Why does God keep this such a secret?"

"Because He saves it for those who watch the night," was my dad's reply.

That winter when the lakes froze over, Dad came home to enjoy a well-deserved rest. While I was home on winter break, the neighborhood amateur horticulturalist came over to tell us that we were in for a big treat that night. And we were instructed to bring our cameras about midnight and meet him in our front yard. Already lacking sleep from final exams, I wondered why God planned all these phenomenal events so early in the morning. But not to disappoint my dad nor miss anything, I agreed to its viewing.

Being curious about this earth-shaking event, cameras in hand, Dad and I again rendezvoused to watch another of God's wonders unfold. Following the sweet odor, we found our neighbor standing at the base of a crooked palm that had stood for years in our front yard. With only moonlight to illuminate the strange-looking plant that had clung to the trunk of that tree, we began to witness our night blooming cereus giving birth. For hours, we stood spellbound while the long spindly petals of the blossom gradually, in slow-motion, unfolded revealing a multitude of delicate yellow-tipped stamens that filled the center and softly swayed with the early morning breeze. It seemed oblivious of its on-lookers or the clicking of their cameras as we attempted to record this breath-taking sight.

It was not difficult to understand why this strangely beautiful blossom was sometimes called "Queen of the Night." After displaying itself wide open, it just as slowly and deliberately began to close its doors to its public.

Dad was right; God saves some of his most mysterious secrets for those who watch the night.

Prayer: *May the stillness and mystery of the night always draw us close to you, and bring peace in our hearts of the promise of your presence in our lives.*

Night Blooming Cereus

Night blooming Cereus, Queen of the Night or **Reina de la noche,** are names of the *Selenicereus grandiflorus,* a cactus originating from Central America, Mexico and the Antilles. It is now native to the Caribbean Islands and found in southern and central Florida. The three-ribbed stem of this strange looking cactus is often found growing on the trunks of trees or climbing on rocks. Sometimes called "Queen of the Night," they begin to produce buds during the summer months, usually in June. The bud will begin to open about 9:00 – 10:00 P.M. and by midnight will be fully open. This phenomenal sight takes place before your eyes like watching a slow motion film. Each bud opens just once and has completed its show and is closed by daybreak.

The cactus has a tuberous, turnip-like root that usually weighs five to fifteen pounds, but has been known to tip the scale at more than one hundred pounds. Native Americans used these roots as a source of food.

There are other lunar-blooming cacti in Florida. One that is prolific in vacant lots and gardens is *Echinopsis pachanoi* or San Pedro cactus. Unlike the night blooming cereus, it is a columnar cactus which sometimes grows to sixteen feet tall. It has from four to nine ribs, most often five to seven. Its large showy blossoms appear at night, and it rarely bears the red tasty fruit.

The stems are used to treat wounds, inflammation, dandruff and fungal skin infections. Because it contains a number of alkaloids, especially mescaline, a psychedelic drug, it is banned from being grown it in some areas where possession of mescaline is illegal. The United States permits its growth, but invokes harsh penalties for manufacturing or sale of the mescaline substance.

To watch either plants bloom is well worth the night watch needed for the show.

> *Even the sparrow has found a home, and the swallow a*
> *nest for herself where she may have her young — a place*
> *near your altar.*

Psalm 84: 3 NIV

Moving from a house on a quarter of an acre of land in Florida to an apartment in the Chicago suburbs was an adjustment, but no garden, that was too much.

After I got my belongings from a four-bedroom house settled into a one-bedroom apartment and converted the dining-L into my office, I headed for the nearest hardware store for "something" on which to grow a garden. I settled on a large set of "do-it-yourself" plastic shelves six feet high.

After much pounding I got the five shelves almost straight and I began filling them with plants. It was spring, the garden shops were abundant, but my budget was scant. So I chose most hardy flowering plants, a few succulents and a large pot of ivy for the very tiptop.

Each day I carefully watered them and talked to them; encouraging them to grow. And they did, especially the pot of ivy. It became full to overflowing, creating a very homey atmosphere. This feeling was apparently shared with others.

I was suddenly aware of a couple of mourning doves sitting on a fence next to the apartment. They seemed to be surveying the scene like a couple of private eyes. Then it seemed that they were making rapid trips to my patio and back, flying with great urgency as though they were on an important mission. And then they disappeared, or so I thought until I reached up with my watering can to give the ivy a morning drink. I was startled when the delicate head of a mourning dove popped out of the ivy and shook off the shower it had just received. It didn't attempt to fly away and looked almost pleadingly at me. I suddenly realized that this couple had chosen my ivy for their birthing place.

Between teaching my classes at the university, grading papers and tending to my household tasks, I kept a careful eye on my newly adopted family. I tried to get home in time to see the male and female change shifts at lunchtime. One day, fearing that the nest had been left unattended, I stood on a chair for a careful inspection. As I quietly approached, the patient parent popped up immediately to protect her expected off-spring. It was evident that they were on duty twenty four-seven.

Occasional gentle rain nourished the ivy, and diligently I waited the big event. One afternoon as I arrived home, I noticed mother dove, sitting on the shelf near her nest, proudly viewing the two scrawny little heads that peered above the pot announcing their arrival with loud chirps.

The second watch was now beginning, as day after day mother dove fed her young until they grew larger and stronger and father took over providing them with a heftier meal. Each day as the couple flew back and forth, they seemed to be demonstrating to their young the art of flying or hedge-hopping.

Then came the day that I had both anticipated and dreaded —

their solo flights. The young spread their wings, proudly imitating their parents, then gave them several pre-flight flapping checks and finally after much urging from mom and dad, they made an enormous first hop of about twenty feet; to the ground; refueled and took off again. After several short flights they arrived on the nearby fence where with several loud chirps they announced to the world the arrival of New Dove Flights One and Two.

With mixed emotions, I bid them good-bye knowing that I had given them a dwelling place from which to be nurtured and grow until they were ready to begin their preparation to become patient parents.

Prayer: Teach us the patience of the dove, who loves and cares for its young the same way you love and care for us.

Ivy — Mourning Dove

Ivy ...

There was a time when every kitchen window had a pot of *Hedera* or English ivy with wallpaper to match. However, to the horticulturalist, English ivy is one of the fifteen species of climbing or ground-creeping evergreen woody plants in the family Araliaceae that are found in gardens in many regions of the world.

Boston Ivy and Virginia creeper, that are also climbers and cling to buildings, are often confused with true ivies, but are really deciduous rather than evergreen and are really related to the grape family.

When shopping for ivy, gardeners are concerned with the size and the shape of the plants as well as the beauty of the leaves. If you are looking for ground cover, an ivy with board leaves such as the English ivy with its large, silvery green, fan-shaped leaves is a favorite. However, to develop a certain mode or design in your garden you might choose "Duck Foot" with its small rounded lobes or "Elegantissma" that produces wide green-gray leaves with white margins. The "Dragon claw" with its large, broad, tightly fluted edges or the "California Fan" with its unusual five to seven, forward-pointing, shallow lobes that curl upward produce lovely effects.

In late autumn ivies produce small greenish-yellow flowers with very rich nectar which is an important food for bees and insects. These are followed by small black berries that ripen in late winter and although poisonous to humans are eaten and dispersed by birds.

It was once believed that climbing ivy damaged houses, however, builders have discovered that strong mortar, especially the more modern substances are not damaged by the clinging roots.

A similar concern was voiced by many gardeners when trees became heavy-laden by climbing ivy. Although the vine may vie for some of the soil's nutrients and water, there doesn't seem to be any cause for concern.

Although not as toxic as its kissing cousin, poison ivy, the English ivy leaves also have toxic qualities.

Like evergreens, ivy is also used as a symbol of eternal life and was often brought into churches to enhance their worship services. Although the Christmas carol, "Holly and the Ivy," seems to revolve around the symbols of Christ found in holly, it is believed that the combination may be representative of male and female with holly having been thought of as the strong, hardy plant and the ivy as the delicate, tender plant.

It seems apparent that the ivy plant has survived the test of time as a gardener's favorite.

The Mourning Dove ...

Growing up in Florida, I was daily greeted in the morning by the "whoo –whoo- call of the mourning dove. This delicate light gray and brown bird is a member of the *Columbidae* family that has also been known as the American Mourning Dove, Rain Dove, Carolina Pigeon and Carolina Turtledove.

This is a very prolific bird. One pair may produce up to six broods a year. Although approximately seventy million are shot annually in the United States, they are still able to maintain a population of approximately four hundred seventy five million.

The male carries on a beautiful courtship beginning with

outstretched wings and head tipped downward in a graceful, circular glide. Upon landing he approaches the female, puffs out his breast, bobs his head while making loud calls. Mated pairs will preen each other's feathers. Doves are monogamous and usually remain pairs, reconvening in the same area the following breeding season and sometimes remain together throughout the winter.

The male leads the female to various sites until she selects one for their nest. As he flies about bringing her material, she builds the nest. Occasionally they will find a nest that they can sublet for their needed stay.

The female usually lays two eggs. Both parents incubate the eggs with the male taking the morning shift and the female the rest of the day and evening. The nest is rarely left unattended for the entire two week period. Although the adults eat mostly seeds, but feed the young crop milk which is a secretion produced in the adult's crop lining. Unlike milk produced for animals, this is a semi-solid substance which the dove regurgitates at the time of the feeding.

Mourning doves are not picky about where they live. They can be found in farm and prairie areas, grasslands, wooded areas and crowded cities. They usually nest in trees, but apparently also like pots of ivy and the rafters of garden shops, as I spotted a pair working on their nest in a Lowe's garden area.

Be still before the Lord, and wait patiently for him.

Psalm 37:7 *NRSV*

It was trying to be spring, but there was still a chill in the air. It started out like any other day— breakfast finished, and the dishes stacked for my husband to take over kitchen duties. I drove the same route to work, hung up my coat and booted up the computer. Coffee cup in hand, I had just finished my morning devotions, when one of the sisters at the convent where I worked entered my office. She didn't stand more than five feet tall. Her black habit touched the ground in the front as her aging shoulders slumped forward. Her deep-set eyes smiled and her outstretched hands offered me a small pot filled with strange-looking green leaves.

"Here, my dear, Happy Birthday," she said in her soft-spoken voice.

"How'd you know?" I replied.

She smiled and pointed heavenward. Because she had access to the convent birthday list, I knew that she hadn't received a divine revelation, but her remembrance was an outpouring of God's love.

Quietly she explained that although it didn't look like much right now, if I would just be patient until Christmas, this little cactus plant would be beautiful.

Expressing by appreciation with a giant hug that almost smothered this tiny saint, I placed it on my bookcase near the window and carefully watered it and watched it, day after day after day. It began to grow, putting out new shoots, but no blossoms. Outside the magnolia trees put on their spring show; the beauty of the sisters' summer flower gardens gave way to the profusion of colored leaves from the oak and maple trees that encircled our grounds. And still my little plant was barren of blossoms. Then just as they began to put away the Thanksgiving decorations and drape the banisters with the evergreens and red bows, I noticed little pink bumps peeking out from the edges of the shiny green leaves. Day by day they grew bigger and brighter and then one morning I opened my office door to behold a most beautiful sight. This tiny plant, dwelling in a simple earthen pot, was arrayed in all its glory. The sunlight illuminated the tiny pink blossoms and flooded the room with such beauty that I rushed to retrieve Sister from her telephone duties so she could share this moment with me.

For more than six decades, sister had given her life to Christ, serving meals to the patients at their hospital, now in her retirement years she served the convent wherever she was needed. She had shared her wealth with me. As we stood together witnessing this magical moment of splendor, she grasped my hand and said,

"Isn't God good to give us such beauty?"

Prayer: *Gracious and loving God, fill us to overflowing with your love. Teach us to share this great gift of love that you have given us with all whom we meet.*

Christmas Cactus

Christmas cactus, Thanksgiving cactus and **Easter cactus** are cousins that belong to the genius *Schlumbergera* often called **zygocactus.** Their differences — the leaves, blossoms and time of year they bloom. They were all originally forest cacti growing at high altitudes in South America. All three plants can be quickly identified by the differences in their leaves and blossoms. The jointed, connected, sectional leaves droop as they grow making them great for hanging baskets; however also making them quite fragile. They can easily break apart when plants are in poor health. These seasonal plants have unbelievably beautiful blossoms in shades of pinks, purples, oranges and white that differ slightly for each plant.

Christmas cactus can be grown from a single segment and planting it into a pot of slightly sandy soil. The plants grow best in a sunlit area and by keeping the soil moist. They bloom once a year and in order to insure their presence at Christmastime, it is important to give the cactus a rest by cutting back on watering (stop watering from October 1 to November) and providing the plant with at least fourteen hours of darkness or until the buds appear. It will then take about ten to twelve weeks to be in full bloom.

Repotting which is best done in the spring, should be done every two to three years.

A Christmas cactus covered with buds, purchased from a garden shop with the expectation of a beautiful holiday display is sometimes disappointing when it begins to shed its blossoms before they open. Changes in temperature, light or lack of water are often the source of this fatal occurrence.

God's Word gives us the meaning of Patience…

Patience is forbearance, endurance, submission, perseverance

Forbearance

> *All have sinned and fall short of the glory of God, and are justified freely by his grace through the redemption that came by Christ Jesus. God presented him as a sacrifice of atonement through faith in his blood. He did this to demonstrate his justice, because in his forbearance he had left the sins committed beforehand unpunished.…*

> Romans 3:23–25 *NIV*

Endurance

> *For everything that was written in the past was written to teach us, so that through endurance and the encouragement of the Scriptures we might have hope. May the God who gives endurance and encouragement give you a spirit of unity among yourselves as you follow Christ Jesus.*

> Romans 15:4–5 *NIV*

Submission

> *But the wisdom that comes from heaven is first of all pure; then peace-loving, considerate, submissive, full of mercy and good fruit, impartial and sincere. Peacemakers who sow in peace raise a harvest of righteousness.*

> James 3:17–18 NIV

Perseverance

> *Therefore, since we are surrounded by such a great cloud of witnesses, let us throw off everything that hinders and the sin that so easily entangles, and let us run with perseverance the race marked out for us. Let us fix our eyes on Jesus, the author and perfecter of our faith, who for the joy set before him endured the cross, scorning its shame, and sat down at the right hand of the throne of God. Consider him who endured such opposition from sinful men, so that you will not grow weary and lose heart.*
>
> Hebrews 12:1–3 *NIV*

> *But the Lord is faithful; he will make you strong and guard you from satanic attacks of every kind. And we trust the Lord that you are putting into practice the things we taught you, and that you always will. May the Lord bring you into an ever deeper understand of the love of God and of the patience that comes from Christ.*
>
> II Thessalonians 3:3–5 *LB*

Seeds of Joy

Satisfy us in our earliest youth with your loving kindness, Giving us constant joy to the end of our lives.

Psalm 90: 14 *LB*

> *He has made everything beautiful in its time. He has*
> *also set eternity in the hearts of men; yet they cannot*
> *fathom what God has done from beginning to end.*
>
> Ecclesiastes 3:11 *NIV*

"Schools out, schools out, teacher let the fools out. No more pencils, no more books, no more teacher's dirty looks," we shouted as we ran down the front steps of our school building on the last day of school.

For me it meant a long, hot, boring summer. Without brothers or sisters, I missed the gathering of friends, classroom activities and the anticipation of something new each day that came with school. However, there was one summer event that filled my vacation with great joy — the bursting into flames of the Royal Poinciana tree.

From my bedroom window, I could see our neighbor's tree. It was the last thing I checked before the sun went down and the first thing my eyes searched for when I awoke. Day by day I watched the huge umbrella of green stretch its arms further and further outward until it was almost as wide as it was tall. Then as it became peppered with buds that resembled miniature green pumpkins, I knew we were in the count down. They grew fatter and fatter, until one morning in mid- June, the tree burst into flames as they popped open to reveal their bright orange blossoms.

For almost the remainder of my summer vacation, I would

climb into the lower limbs and sit on my royal throne pretending that I was the queen in her castle. I'd adorn my braids with blossoms that fell to the ground and order the birds and bugs that flew by to carry out my commands. In the evening I would fill the pages of my drawing pads with a struggling young artist's renderings of the tree.

Then as my vacation days sadly came to an end, my royal castle closed for another year.

As the summers went by, I traded my pretend castle for the wonderland of books.

One summer, I met Jenny Totten who marched right out of the pages of Theodore Pratt's *Flame Tree.* This was the exciting tale of a young couple who ventured from Ohio to Florida during the fabulous early Flagler Days. This beautiful young woman found herself married to a hunter, living in a cabbage house made from palmetto fronds and driftwood that was built next to "her tree" — a magnificent Royal Poinciana.

Page after page, I waited with her for the tree to burst into flames. This was her Shangri-la, that filled her barren surroundings with great joy.

For Jenny, the division of the classes on the two sides of the lake became a reality. The elegance of the people that the railroad brought to the fabulous Royal Poinciana Hotel and simplicity of the "crackers" who picked the crops and did the household tasks were as widely separated as were the differences of the beach dwelling's well-coiffured gardens of bougainvillea and stately royal palms and the citrus trees mingled among the saw palmetto and banyan trees on the inland side.

And a half century later, as I read about the struggles of these settlers in a new and wild frontier, I realized that this tree still represents the joy of anticipation.

Prayer: *Lord, we are grateful for every drop of rain that falls, for every star that lights the sky and for every tree that blossoms brightly because they bring us the joy that comes from your love.*

Royal Poinciana

Delonix regia, Flame, Flamboyant, Kirshnachura, Gulmohar, Peacock Flower, Royal Poinciana tree, whatever name you give it, cannot fully describe the beauty of this magnificent tree.

A member of the *Fabaceae* family, the Royal Poinciana is a large ornamental tree sometimes reaching forty feet tall with widely spreading branches that often reach out wider than the tree's height. The fern-like loose leaves make excellent shade while still allowing a breeze to filter through them. In the early non-air conditioned days of Florida, they were planted for shade and beauty. Although deciduous in some areas, in the moist climate of Florida, they tend to be semi-evergreen.

Once a year the tree earns its name, flamboyant or flame tree. As the green mini-pumpkin looking buds open and the orange-red blossoms cover the tree giving the appearance of being on fire.

The flowers have four spoon shaped petals and one upright that is slightly larger, with yellow and white markings. Each individual flower resembles a tiny orchid.

It is a very fast growing tree which can increase about five feet per year until its maturity. However, it has shallow wide-spread root system that can be a threat to building foundations and sidewalks.

It produces a flat dark brown seed pod that may reach twenty-four inches in length and in the Caribbean Islands is called "woman's tongue" because of the rattling noise they make when blown by the wind.

This tree is so well-loved that it has influenced the naming of numerous historical places in Florida, especially in the Palm Beach area.

Ponce de Leon, who was supposedly searching for waters that would bring eternal youth, is credited with the discovery of Florida in 1513. However, Florida's development proceeded slowly with Spain, Britain and Spain again taking command before it became the 27ᵗʰ state in 1845.

During the late nineteenth century, Florida emerged as a popular tourist destination. Henry Flagler, an oil, real estate and railroad tycoon, fell in love with Florida's east coast and began buying all the tracts of land that were available in the late 1800s especially around his beloved Palm Beach. As his Florida East Coast Railroad pushed its way southward, he built five luxurious hotels from Jacksonville to Miami. Possibly his favorite was the Royal Poinciana Hotel, built in 1894 on the island of Palm Beach. This Georgian-style hotel which was the largest wooden structure in the world at the time was as magnificent as its namesake. Flagler spared no expense making his guests welcome and comfortable in Palm Beach, the town he founded.

A small group of worshipers under the leadership of Rev. Alexander B. Dilley, that had been meeting in homes and a school, attracted Flagler's attention. To provide his hotel guests a lovely place to worship, he donated the land and money for the building of the four hundred-seat Royal Poinciana Chapel, completed in 1898. Because the Royal Poinciana Hotel guests were of many different denominations, Flagler wanted the church to serve a variety of denominations. The chapel has been moved several times and is now located at 60 Cocoanut Row in Palm Beach near Whitehall, the Henry Morrison Flagler Home and present museum.

Many other places in South Florida pay tribute to this magnificent tree and bear its name.

A happy heart makes the face cheerful, but heartache cruses the spirit.

Proverbs 15:13 *NIV*

Growing up on the coast of South Florida, as a teenager, I belonged to the society of "beach bums." In our small hometown, as soon as we were old enough to ride our bikes to school, we were liberated and allowed to venture across the Intracoastal Waterway that separated the mainland from the "beach."

During our teen years, when we became too sophisticated to ride our bikes, we girls walked, hoping to be picked up by a guy with a motor bike. And the symbol of young manhood was a motorbike.

The beach was our second home. We climbed down the dunes to a spot near the surf; put down our blankets and staked our claim to an area for the gathering of our high school friends. Even on windy days when the waves were high and the sand blowing, we could find a spot where the growth of sturdy sea grapes, waving sea oats and blossoming yucca or Spanish bayonet, as we called them, provided a protective barrier. The taxonomy and nomenclature of these seaside plants was not of interest to us. The guys were only interested in gathering some yucca sword-shaped leaves to use as darts to aim at the girls' derrieres, which was their method of saying, "I like you." And the girls simply enjoyed the beauty of their waxy white blossoms as we sat and wove sea oats stems into chains and pretended to ignore the boys.

These were joyous gatherings, filled with laughter and fun. The beach and its surroundings were an equalizing territory for us. What side of town you came from; what your daddy did for a living, where you bought your bathing suit (which was usually the only clothing item we had that wasn't homemade) was not important. We all went to one high school, we all gathered on one beach – our beach.

We graduated and went our separate ways. The years turned into decades and I'm sure all of us often thought of the hours we had spent at the beach.

I ended up in Chicago, where winter comes early and stays late. Married to a Chicago-boy, it was difficult to describe our joyous beach gatherings and how I occasionally missed them. Until one spring, while wading through the backyard slush on my way to the garbage can, I spied a plant in the neighbor's backyard that had defied the elements and decided to bloom. This spike of white blossoms looked so out of place in its desolate surroundings. Unable to believe my eyes, I retrieved the binoculars from the house and returned to reassure myself that it wasn't a wishful mirage. There it was, a yucca, in the spring, in Chicago, with no golden sand, no ocean waves to nourish it. It was one of the biggest and most beautiful blossoms I'd ever seen. Or maybe it just appeared that way on a chilly spring day.

I quickly dragged my reluctant, protesting husband to the back steps, handed him the binoculars and insisted that he view this, the eighth wonder of the world. He focused and then refocused and gazed for several long minutes before turning to me and asking, "What did you say it is? It grows where?"

I started to give an excited, non-stop, scientific explanation combined with another recounting of my beach days, when he interrupted, took another sighting and replied, "That's incredible."

Somehow I knew that he, too, felt the warmth of the sun, heard the roar of the sea and envisioned the beauty of the ocean shore that had brought me such joy.

Prayer: Lord, you bring us unexpected and undeserved joy with the all your creation. Teach me to share this joy. Help us remember the lessons learned from fellowship with friends.

Yucca (Spanish Bayonet)

The yucca plants belongs to the *Agavaceae* family which has more than forty species of these perennials shrubs. They are found in North and Central America and the West Indies.

They are grown as ornamental plants because of their lovely large white blossoms and sharp pointed bushy leaves that have made them popular as hedge plants.

They have an unusual method of pollination. The yucca moth carries the pollen of one plant to the stigma of another; then lays an egg in the flower from which the larva emerges to eat some of the seeds, but not all.

Yuccas have many edible parts — fruit, seeds, flowers and stems but they are not to be confused with the completely unrelated, "yuca" or cassava plant which produces the starchy flour that makes tapioca.

One of the species, the *Yucca aloifolia* better known as the

Spanish bayonet or dagger plant, is a guardian of the beaches from North Carolina south through Florida. Their ability to withstand high winds makes them right at home along coastal sand dunes and the margins of brackish marshes. Evergreen all year, they bloom from May to June, and their seeds ripen in September.

Besides adding beauty and intrigue to any landscape, they are both edible and useful. Their fruit and flowers can be eaten both raw and cooked, the flower's stem is often peeled and boiled and used like asparagus. Fiber from the leaves is used in making rope, baskets and mats; the leaf splints have been used as brushes to paint pottery, and the roots are rich in saponins that can be used as a substitute for soap.

God hath made me laugh, so that all that hear will laugh with me.

Genesis 21: 6 *KJV*

Hearing the chatter of a familiar unwanted garden guest, I rushed to the window to view a squirrel scurrying up the squirrel-proof pole of my new squirrel-proof bird feeder.

I raced from the house to inform this little rascal that the birds trying to visit my well-planned bird-attracting garden would starve if he kept stealing their food. Quite unimpressed, he took his time munching on the sunflower seeds before departing to raid another feeder.

I was exasperated. I had tried every new gadget on the market that promised to keep squirrels from the bird food. "God sure goofed when he created squirrels" I muttered under my breath as I walked off fuming at my defeat.

The next day as I gazed out my office window, I saw the elderly man from the nursing home next door, leaning on his three-pronged cane and shuffling slowly down the pathway between our buildings. He frequently came and sat on a bench that was shaded by a huge old oak tree. He usually just sat for a while, staring into space and then shuffled back to his place of confinement. I was just about to take my break and go out to sit with him when I noticed him opening a small paper bag that he had placed on the bench. He took out a peanut, cracked it open and popped it into his mouth with a resigned motion, almost as though he had been ordered to eat his morning snack.

In a few minutes, to my surprise, a frisky little squirrel hopped up on the bench beside him. It stood on its hind legs, flicked its tail and chattered loudly trying to get the old gentleman's attention. Finally in desperation, it stuck its head into the bag and came out with a prize reward. The old man watched it as it devoured the peanut and then headed for another. Cautiously, the gentleman handed his guest his next selection which the squirrel accepted and devoured. He handed him another and another. As the squirrel accepted his offerings, munched and begged for one more, a smile crept across the old gentleman's face which escalated into laughter. Suddenly his laughter could be heard above the rustle of the drying leaves overhead.

Staying until the bag was empty, they both chatted and shared the morning snack. Finally the old gentleman rose to return to his residence. As he headed down the pathway there was a little more spring to his step. He stopped, turned and waved good-bye to his new friend, but I'm sure that they had made a date to meet again tomorrow.

Prayer: *Lord, remind us that each of us is important to you. Help us to see the joy that we can bring to others when we stop to share our gifts.*

Squirrel

The common ground squirrel belongs to the family *Sciuridae.* The name comes from the Greek word *skiouros,* meaning shadow-tailed, because of the way they use their tail to shade their entire body. This is a rather large family having two hundred and seventy eight species and fifty-one genera making it one of the most diverse families of mammals. It includes the grey squirrel, flying squirrels, terrestrial marmots, chipmunks, prairie dogs and a terrestrial and tree squirrels.

Red squirrels are found from Alaska across Canada, the northeast states and southward through the Appalachian states. Enjoyed for their beautiful red coloring, they like to live in old woodpecker holes, tree hollows, and small crevices. When migrating to find winter food, they will often cross water and are good swimmers.

My fascination still exists with the white and albino squirrel. Although they appear to be the same, the albino squirrel has a recessive gene that limits the pigmentation all over including the skin, feet and hands and produces pink eyes. White squirrels will have dark eyes. These squirrels seem to inhabit certain areas and five cities lay claim to being home of the albino squirrel — Oleny, Illinois; Brevard, North Carolina; Marionville, Missouri; Kenton, Tennessee and Exeter, Ontario.

Students at the University of North Texas fell in love with their only albino squirrel and until its death by a hungry hawk believed that if you saw the squirrel before an exam it would bring luck. Now I guess they have to study.

Olney, Illinois, known as the Home of the White Squirrel, really goes all out for their critters, protecting them with laws of right-of-way on the streets and forbidding them to be transported out of the city.

Unable to digest cellulose like many other mammals, squirrels rely on foods rich in protein, carbohydrates and fat. Therefore, they love to raid the garden of planted bulbs, tree buds, pine cones and nuts and steal food from bird feeders.

Squirrels are used for meat in certain regions of the United States. Finding it difficult to dine on when served at an outdoor conference, my husband reminded me that cows have sad brown eyes and can be quite loveable, so I should close my eyes and eat. I couldn't.

You have let me experience the joys of life and the exquisite pleasures of your own eternal presence.

Psalm 16: 11 *LB*

It was the summer of 1951, shortly after the pomp and circumstance of my high school graduation had faded away. I boarded the Great Lakes cargo freighter that my father sailed for my usual summer vacation. This had been my summer activity since I was a toddler, but this summer was different in so many ways. It would be my last summer that I would spend at sea with my dad. In the fall, I would be off to college, and future summers would be spent working.

Many of the young men from my class had their college plans postponed while they headed for a far-off land to defend people in a politically divided country.

My dad and his crew had been the first boat that season to ply the cold and dangerous waters of Lake Superior. It had been a trip laden with left-over ice and high seas. It had taken several months before they could enjoy the warmth of summer.

Climbing the mid-ship ladder, I was greeted by my dad, several sailors whom I had come to know as family, and **petunias!** Petunias! Growing in snow-white painted scrub- buckets and homemade flower boxes, they adorned the usually sterile bridge and pilothouse and various other spots on the ship. There were big ones, small ones and ruffled ones. They were pink, white, purple, and two-toned. And it seemed they were everywhere.

Fearing the ship might be renamed the SS Reluctant, my father might be labeled Capt. Morton and the crew might mutiny at any minute, I quickly admired them and asked how they got all the petunias. The immediate answer came from a gruff-voiced seaman,

"Ya, ain't they beautiful, they're the captain's" (usually referred to as the old man, but not in his presence).

After I was dragged forward to inspect the blossoms, my dad hastened to assure me that he really wasn't experiencing a "senior moment." He went on to explain that spring on shore is colorful and promising, but at sea it is still dreary and drab. The leftover ice and gray skies still feel threatening.

On his first trip ashore, the streets were filled with vendors selling their flowers. The bright colors were such a joyous sight that it reminded him of our gardens at home. He had only planned to buy a few for his quarters, but they were all so beautiful he had difficulty making a selection, so he filled the trunk of his waiting taxi. He confessed that he received several questioning glances from the crew, but a few off-watch crew members caught the flower-bug and began painting scrub buckets and making flower boxes from old packing crates. With a shrug of his shoulders and a wink, he confessed that their garden just seemed to grow.

That summer the crew seemed to be wearing more smiles than usual and some even whistled as they went about their work.

Although dad got a lot of ribbing from comrades on passing ships, the next summer an armada of freighters joined the Great

Lakes Garden Club. Perhaps that's why I always save a spot in my garden for a bed of petunias.

Prayer: *Father, you fill our hearts with joy with the simplest things in life. Let's us remember to share this joy with every passer-by.*

Petunia

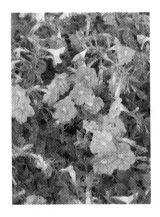

Although it may be difficult to spot the resemblance between **Petunias** and tobacco, they all belonging to the *Solanaceae* family, along with potatoes and tomatoes. The name petunia comes from the French word *petun,* originally taken from the Tupin-Guarani language meaning tobacco.

With the coming of the first warmth of spring, gardeners flock to nurseries to purchase their petunias. It is not surprising that they have remained one of the top five selling bedding plants for over one hundred years.

Two cultivars or varieties were natives of South America and are believed to be the ancestors of modern petunias. In 1880 Mrs. Theodosia Shepherd brought to California the *Superbissima* type of petunia. With careful cultivating this developed into the *grandiflora* and *multiflora* that are today's biggest sellers in our garden shops.

The multiflora was developed in the late 1940s. They are a hardy, rapid-growing plant available in a wide variety of colors. The grandiflora petunia was developed in the early 1950s and was the variety that decorated the S.S. Perseus in the summer of 1951. They produce both single and double blossoms that come in a wide variety of colors and designs— solid and bi-color, deep veined, striped and with contrasting edges. The double-flower forms have ruffled petals and resemble carnations.

New colors and varieties are always being developed and two of the newest and most popular varieties are the spreading and the milliflora petunias. The **wave petunia**, has become "all the **rave** of a petunia." Developed to be a spreading, trailing plant, they are great for borders, hanging planters and flower boxes. The milliflora is a miniature petunia whose flowers are about thirty-six percent the size of the multifloras. They bloom earlier and are more tolerant of all types of weather conditions.

Because all petunias are cultivated from seed, some gardeners like to brave it and start theirs from seed.

Wherever placed in the garden, petunias always make a happy spot that brings joy to both gardener and visitors.

> *Charm is deceptive, and beauty is fleeting; but a woman*
> *who fears the Lord is to be praised.*

Proverbs 31:30 *NIV*

It had been fifty years since we walked down the aisle of our high school auditorium to receive a piece of paper proving we had completed the course of study prescribed by the state of Florida.

One by one we began to gather. Arriving by plane from far away, or automobile from just around the corner, we assembled to share the memories of growing up in a small southern town where no one locked their doors and everyone knew who walked you home after the game.

I recognized some classmates right away and for others I was relieved when we put on our nametags. We were all a little more gray and most a little more plump than we had been the last time we met. It seemed amazing that almost half of our class of eighty-six had gathered half a century later.

Because there were only three elementary schools in town and one junior-senior high school, many of us had been pals since first grade.

For months before I flew from Chicago, I had shown my husband outfits in store windows and in catalogs, looking for the one that was going to make me look younger than the rest of the gang. My husband lovingly reminded me that we were all the same age, as he finally pointed to the ensemble that he said was going to do it. As I stared at the chiffon skirt and linen jacket in a very unusual shade of pink, I questioned if he was sure this would do the job. I was a brown, tan or maybe rust person, but pink? "It's a winner, it's you," he assured me. So there I was standing in the nametag line in my new outfit hoping that no one sensed how much my feet hurt, when I felt a tap on my shoulder. Turning around, I stood face to face, with one of my best friends from grade school.

"When I saw someone dressed in sticky-flower pink, I knew it had to be you." A few hugs and tears later, we grabbed a seat and started to catch up on decades of living. When our storytelling slowed, I inquired what she meant by "sticky-flower pink." Don't you remember how on the way home from grade school we picked those beautiful little sticky flowers and made jewelry out of them?"

How could I have forgotten? Our elementary school years were also "the war years." Living in a coastal community meant black-out conditions; beach patrols watching for unfriendly planes; and siblings in faraway places. We bought savings stamps, collected scrap metal and entertained ourselves. Making sticky-flower jewelry provided hours of fun. We would pick the delicate white with pinkish trim flowers. They were so sticky a single blossom could be placed on our earlobes for earrings, or lined up around our necks to form a lovely necklace. Our custom designs were second only to Tiffany. We probably looked silly, but we felt like queens.

As we parted after that joyous celebration, I wondered if we'd ever meet again and if there were still "sticky flowers" in the few open fields left along the highly developed Gold Coast of Florida. Sadly because there don't seem to be, little girls won't have the joy of being "queen for moment" bejeweled with sticky tarflowers.

Prayer: Lord, may we always have the joy of childhood to heal the hurts of life. Help us to see life through the eyes of a child and love with the devotion of a friend.

Tarflower

In the vacant lots of south Florida before developers cleared the land for high-rise condos, there dwelt the lovely *Bejaria racemosa (Befaria racemosa)* a member of the *Ericaceae* or heath family. They were known to native Floridians as tarflower, fly catcher or sticky flower.

There kissing cousins in the *Ericaceae* or heath family were mostly lime-hating plants that thrived on acid soils. These relatives were azaleas, rhododendrons, heather and even cranberries and blueberries. Most of these plants live in temperate climates, however, there are several tropical species, thus the tarflower which grew everywhere in Florida. I say "grew" because as vacant sand lots disappeared, so has the tarflower.

Tarflowers, or sticky flowers as children often called them, are beautiful, delicate white to pinkish flowers that are very fragrant and very sticky having, six to seven petals. They are found on woody shrubs in the scrub woods of Florida, Alabama and Georgia. Blooming from April to September, the sweet fragrance attracts insects, and their sweet nectar is a food for butterflies. However, their sticky petals often trap flies and other insects.

You will both have great joy and gladness at his birth,
and many will rejoice with you.

Luke 1: 14 *LB*

Sometimes you have to be careful where you step in your garden. Landing on an ant hill, I quickly retrieved my stinging foot, drenched it with water and noted that my disturbance caused pain to both me and the ants.

The usually organized pattern of marching in and out of their hill had turned into utter chaos and confusion as they rushed about much in the same way my sixth grade students reacted the day of the school's gigantic Christmas program.

The Christian Academy where I taught was noted for their Christmas production. Renting an auditorium that seated several thousand, the students spent weeks practicing their music, memorizing their speaking parts and painting the background panels that they were required to mathematically enlarge from an assigned picture. The music, dramatic presentations and even the processional and recessional were rehearsed until they were next to perfection.

The day began with five hundred plus students — junior kindergarten through senior high — being bused to the auditorium for one last rehearsal with props, costumes, orchestra and choruses. Returning to school, lunch was even cut short so we could make it to our afternoon classes on time.

I looked at my thirty-six exhausted students that were wound like rubber bands, all wanting to do their very best, but fearful that they would mess up. This was our last day together before Christmas break. That night they would arrive in full uniform, would be on their best behavior, would sing their hearts out; then we would go to our separate homes to await the celebration of the birth of Christ. Christ who came into the world as a tiny baby, who was sung to by his mother, whose birth was celebrated by the animals that shared his dwelling. I wanted them to feel the love that was felt that night by a family chosen to witness this wonderful event.

After promising that all would receive an "A" on the scheduled spelling test, I suggested that we push our desks back; sit down on the floor and share a moment together. They begged me to read to them. Wondering what I had to share, I suddenly remembered the little book I had brought days before but no spare time to read it had ever become available. Leaning against the wall or propped up by a desk, they began to relax as I read from a little sermon preached more than twenty years before by Peter Marshall, a minister from Scotland. His message reminded us that through all the hub-bub and new fangled things that we create to try to improve our the celebration of Christ's birth, there is really only one true message — "God so loved the world that he gave his only Son, so that everyone who believes in him may not perish but may have eternal life." (John 3: 16). In the closing lines from his book, he suggested that, "We should not "**spend**" Christmas, nor "**observe**" Christmas, but "**Keep**" Christmas in our hearts.

I closed the book and placed it in my lap as the voice of one student rang out with a simple song – "Jesus loves me this I know," and one by one each of us joined in as we took hands and began to sing. One praise song followed another until our room was filled with the joyous sound of praise to the Lord.

That night my class was never more radiant, never more sincere as they sat proudly in their section and sang every note and recited every line right on cue. When we shared our hugs and shouted our Merry Christmas good-byes there were thirty-six, make that thirty-seven students who had witnessed the joy of celebrating the birth of Jesus.

Prayer: *May the wonder of Your gift to us, Jesus, fill us with such great joy that it is reflected in all that we do and all that we say throughout each day the whole year through.*

Garden Ants

Ants in the kitchen, ants on the sidewalk, ants in the garden, sometimes we think that ants are everywhere. And with more than twelve thousand species of these social insects belonging to the family *Formicidae,* they are everywhere.

Easily identified by their elbowed antennae and the node-like structure that forms their slender waist, they are frequent visitors to our gardens.

Although some ants are nomadic and wander about, many ants build complex structures varying from simple mounds of sand to stronger mounds made from a mixture of sticks and dirt that offer greater protection from the rain. The Western Harvester ant makes a small mound on top of the surface and then tunnels to about fifteen feet straight down to hibernate during the winter. Most ant homes are designed with different chambers providing them with nurseries, food storage areas, and resting places.

These simple creatures have exoskeletons with three main parts: head, trunk and the rear or metasoma. Although they have rather poor eyesight, their prominent eyes are made of many lenses which allow them to see movement, necessary to stay alive. They do most of their work with their antennae that provide them with smell, touch, taste and hearing. Without a heart they rely on a long perforated tube that runs along the top of their body to circulate internal fluids.

Ants communicate by touching their antennae and leaving a scented trail for other ants to follow. Step on an anthill and you will quickly discover that they defend themselves by biting or stinging their enemy by injecting or spraying them with a chemical like folic acid. Fire ants have been known to kill birds or small animals. Every year about 20 million people are stung by fire ants.

Ginger Schmidt

Be Joyful

Let the heavens rejoice, let the earth be glad; let them say among the nations,

"The Lord reigns!"

Let the sea resound, and all that is in it;

Let the fields be jubilant, and everything in them!

Then the trees of the forest will sing,

The will sing for joy before the Lord,

For he comes to judge the earth

Give thanks to the Lord, for he is good;

His loves endures forever.

I Chronicles 16:31–34

From the Psalms...

Shout with joy to God, all the earth!

Sing the glory of his name;

Make his praise glorious

Psalm 66:1–2 *NIV*

Let the nations be glad and sing for joy,

For you judge the peoples with equity

And guide the nations upon the earth... *Selah*

Psalm 67:4 *NRSV*

Shout for joy to the Lord, all the earth.

Worship the Lord with gladness; come before him with joyful songs.

Know that the Lord is God.

It is he who made us and we are his

We are his people, the sheep of his pasture.

Enter his gates with thanksgiving and his courts with praise;

Give thanks to him and praise his name.

For the Lord is good and his love endures forever;

His faithfulness continues through all generations.

Psalm 100 *NIV*

The Author

Ginger Schmidt is the daughter of a Great Lakes Captain, who grew up and taught school in Florida before moving to Chicago where she met her late husband, Bob Schmidt, author and editor.

She holds a Bachelor of Arts in Elementary Education and history from Stetson University, Florida and a Master of General Studies in journalism from Roosevelt University, Chicago.

She taught public and private school, and designed and taught creative writing courses for the Adult Education Program in Palm Beach County, Florida. She also served as an admissions counselor at several universities in Illinois as well as teaching English at Roosevelt University, Chicago.

For more than a decade, her column "Camping Comforts," as well as numerous travel articles, have appeared in outdoor magazines and newspapers in the U.S.

She is also the compiler of *Freebies for Cat Lovers* (Prince Paperbacks, Crown Publisher, Inc). and publisher of *Have They Heard You, Lord?* (GinMak Communications, Inc.); co-author of *Great Lakes Circle Tour: Reliving History Along Lake Michigan's Circle Tour Route* (Palmer Publications, Amherst Press) and *Great Lake Camping* (Foghorn Outdoors, Avalon Travel).

She has two sons, Jim and Rick, four grandchildren and three great-grandchildren. She currently resides in Avon Park, Florida where she is active at Emmanuel United Church of Christ.

The Photographer

Glen Shellhammer retired from teaching, coaching, and sponsoring high school students in 2002.

He then started his own photography business photographing weddings, events, nature, and sports.

His love of photography had sprung from his involvement in the high school yearbook publishing that he sponsored for fifteen years. During this time he built darkrooms, taught photographic skills, and developed and printed photos for the school's yearly edition.

In 2000 he converted his photo and text coverage to the digital format and produced for the next two years a digitally submitted book.

Since retirement he has focused his love of photography in his business, *Focus on You Photography*, and continued to hone his skills in digital enhancement in Photoshop. He can be reached by snail mail at 3549 East Gleneagles Drive, Avon Park, Florida 33825 and at glenshellhammer@aol.com on the internet.